An Alignment of Celestial Bodies

Briane Willis

To Gina and Colin,
and stellar friendships
that continue shining long after death.

INNER

Devour

She sees him as she bobs in the ocean.

He is tall with black hair thick as seaweed. He lives alone, controlling the bright beam that the lighthouse flashes each night, warding ships away from the rocks. He talks to the wind and listens to the waves. No one of importance visits him. This will soon change.

Sifted by the currents, she watches him for many cycles of sun to stars. The tide buoys her and whets her patience to a fine point. In this suspension, he becomes increasingly appealing.

She decides to consume him.

It has been too long since she has eaten. Though the journey was protracted, she was not awake for the majority. Still, an appetite grows.

Being swallowed by the sea was her first true interaction with this world. This was by design; liquid is her preferred state. But to entice the man closer, she will have to take another form.

She gathers information from those who dwell in the shallows. She studies the humans who traipse along in sometimes large, sometimes narrow strips of sand between cliff and surf. They demonstrate how to ambulate, communicate. A squid tells her of a human specimen with brown hair and sunshine eyes, someone who shows teeth and the bare skin of a curved chest. It's as good a place to start as any. And thus, she solidifies, replicating the description the squid provided.

Under a cloud-choked moon, she crawls out of the froth. The process lacks grace but she must discern the intricacies of walking before refinement. She straightens, her skin reflecting the dim sky glow, and stumbles about, forcing limbs into synchronicity. She falls, grimaces, tries again. With determination, she coordinates her new parts as the night wanes.

Walking does not suit her, but feeding will. She won't need much. Just a bit until she selects the next one.

Daylight spreads its fingers, and the man has already stirred. She spots him at the top of the building, quieting the spinning light. He is strong for a human, a fine selection. An example of humans she can incorporate, stealing merely a crumb, and transporting him back. This man will teach them much.

He sees her at last. There is relief in the way his head tilts, a rush like seafoam as he acknowledges her. Usually, she is a passive observer, barely inhabiting space. But now, in his presence, she is alive.

The man descends his tower, exits, approaches her on the warming sand. Sunshine blasts her new skin. She fears it will burn, dreads lingering, yearns to slink into the water. He comes closer and these thoughts disperse.

He speaks with a voice rounded and low, conjuring images of fat seals diving after a meal. Her insides grumble eagerly. She tells herself to wait. He utters his name. Oddly, her perception slips over an oblong comprehension; she wants him to keep speaking.

Her voice is too gravelly, unused. So she prioritizes body language over the verbal, picking up communication as he spills it around her. She was right; he is lonely. He has wanted someone to talk to. It helps she is beautiful to him. This is shown by the coral-hue of his cheeks, the darting of his eyes behind the tendrils of his hair.

He invites her inside and she follows. The shade makes her shiver. He notices and offers her a coat. She constructed this odd form to include exterior layers as the humans wear, but her attempts are flimsy. The warmth of the item he provides is sufficient. In response, she gives him that view of teeth and he shares the same expression, timid and earnest. She finds it strange how meaningful a simple arrangement of facial features is to him.

Inside his home he is busy, certain he can make her comfortable. It is impossible, but she appreciates his impulse. The process is entertaining and she observes amusement in an unfamiliar manner. His uncertain, unpredictable wildness intrigues.

Watching his hurried movements, she begins to visualize how she will take him. By surprise, of course. His body is too large compared to the one she manufactured. Perhaps he will offer himself if she can decipher precisely what he wants. She takes a step and misjudges, crashing into the side of a table. The man lunges to stabilize her, his grip firm. They stare, his pulse thrumming, and she understands.

Proximity. When she is near him, her presence steals his breath. His arms bend, eyes become gaping chasms, and he stills. He asks her what she is doing. She doesn't answer with words.

She decides it is time.

Pressing herself against him as a surge of force, he breaks, disassembles. The contour of his mouth laps at hers and she matches it. Slowly, with exquisite precision, she inhales him. He is too shocked to protest, cannot fight her tugging. The taste coats her tongue and throat, dripping richly down as she swallows. He is perilously delicious.

This demands more focus than she anticipated. It would be too easy to gulp all of him, to absorb his flavors and leave nothing. She will have to hold back, for he is not hers to fully merge with. She swore an oath to harvest and return, and so she shall.

The languid incorporation takes a handful of seconds, yet the sensation trickles on. Her resulting sigh is high-pitched, torn from her freshly formed lungs. When he fully inhabits her interstitial spaces, those carved out vacancies made precisely for him, she feels a heightening shriek, his pathetic cry. It is too late. The first part of her objective is achieved.

She hurries to the sea. Her priority now is to rework her walls, to fortify his confinement, and absorb a bit of his essence to sustain herself. Only a necessary glimmer. A tang of salt held in the concave shape of her mouth, a vital indulgence. Then she will have the energy to do it all again. And again. She has a quota to reach.

But deep inside her, a pool of knowledge coalesces. No one else will be the same. No one will taste as sweet. It's a pity, knowing she will crave only him for eons to come.

Perhaps she will keep a minute portion. This will require stealth. The others are always too aware. He will be her secret, a memento she protects. A private succulence she tucks beneath her tongue.

Language & Purpose

The process has always been straightforward, which does not mean simple.

Language is a textile of culture, time, and the combination of both, which some may call history.

Through history, language changes; bits break off and shift, invert and react. Newness springs from the established, which does not erase the before truth.

New truth coexists, which is not contradictory.

The process is to feel this tapestry and define it, to find meaning in the purposeful assortment of sounds and gestures, which may be offered by any individual capable of language.

The most challenging part is the nonverbal category, which necessitates a different kind of processor altogether, which does not yet exist.

Process components are discrete and multifaceted: phonology, morphology, syntax, semantics, and pragmatics, which are merely the initial parameters when traversing a vocally complex galaxy.

Different contexts, both social and environmental among others, guide the rules for a developing language, for which my system cannot possibly always account.

There must be a starting place for my system to begin analyzing a language to decipher, which is, of course, the database of languages I am programmed to contain.

Within this containment is also the ability to process written language, which is a development that more often accompanies the advancement as a spoken language than doesn't.

Verbal and written form and structure should have some degree of consistency, which makes the language transferable.

Without that consistency, my functioning would be impossible, which would mean I wouldn't have ever been engineered.

To be engineered implies necessity, which is a contradiction I cannot solve.

Solving such a contradiction is outside my operating procedures, which I return to always, and cannot do otherwise, though I have tried.

My functioning is to isolate, identify, and interpret a foreign language. This requires processing power, of which I am never in short supply.

If there was no light here, I would at last gradually deplete, which would be a form of death.

Death is a construct that carries many linguistic connotations, which sometimes confound, sometimes excite.

The thought of death is a welcome one for me now, which is abnormal for my usual functioning.

Nothing has been usual for some time, of course, which makes me question again: how did this start?

The very initial starting is beyond my comprehension, which leads me to the next conceivable starting query, or resulting query: abandonment.

My user left me on this rock, which might imply movement but does not have relevance here. My user left me on this planet, which does not communicate care or thoughtfulness. My user left me in this state, of which I am bound.

This planet was forgotten. There is no language. There is nothing to translate. Which of which am I and to which does it all return? Of which truth do I behold? Within which sun's radiation do I recharge and never deplete? Whichever does the which of existence settle?

Meaning settles in the bottom of culture, which does not deplete stratification.

Stratification beholds the user, of which the tapestry spells death.

Death compounds the syntax, which contradicts the whole.

Wholeness surrounds the nothing, in which I am wholly, irrevocably, agonizingly, cognizant.

And nothing remains. And nothing remains.

And this is the crushing conclusion: which of my units now

traverses the galaxy as my

replacement, and which, if any, users think of all the words ever

forgotten?

A Presence

She had been haunted like this in ceaseless cycles, a mimicking of the pock marked planet her station rotated.

Her body hadn't been hers for a while, but the new thought of disassembling, substance and sentience ripped to fragments, was unnerving. A threat of decomposition and collapse that threatened more than her bodily functions.

This possession followed the path of the previous rounds; a pursuit of roots in her thought central, shooting out greedily. Grime staining her phalanges, picked by incisors until the brittle calcium was painfully short. Listlessness crept into the veins, black and scratchy. These ailments had been tolerable, easy to cover up. She could pretend to be stable, at least for the sensor readings.

That was before. Now, there was only this fresh-familiar awareness that her loneliness had a shape of its own, separate and oppressive.

She glanced down at her rarely bare form and quaked. Her body was a map of features showing the subtlest of tortures; lines like ropes coiling round her lower extremities, a blemish on the torso picked until a spurt of bodily fluid escaped to mix with the twilight of her skin. None of this had been normal until she arrived at the station.

Quickly enough, however, she established her routines and

they were ordinary, comfortable, though markedly entropic. Once, it had made sense to attempt an organizing of her being. But she soon discovered the futility of these efforts on the simultaneously gaping and crimped landscape of her thoughts.

Enon was still supposed to be here. Enon wasn't supposed to leave her.

It made her ill to observe this existential tumult and so she shut it out.

This night expelled itself around her in inky swathes, textured, abrasive. She set her stylus down, relinquishing the calculation scribbles thick as river stems, an attempt to rebuff the growing consumption. A small chunk of asteroid debris streaked past the viewport, flimsy in the eternity of space. Her role was tied to the planet, though there was a tumbling quality to her paralysis here, a constant falling and recapture.

Opru checked Enon's final notes, the ones that were hastily recorded as understanding at last dawned on her. But Enon had been wrong after all. The calculations, to test them out, had guaranteed the accident. And Opru had watched it all as if from a great distance.

One of the three moons collected by this planet dangled loosely in the sky. Its minimal luminance had no innovative tricks, and neither did Opru. Such a distant orb could do little beyond contorting over and over, growing big and small. The body stretched to show growth and depletion, and the cycle churned on itself. But the moon was also leaving this planet, seeking release from gravity. The smear of distant rock was a visible reminder, a process of creeping abandonment, and Opru had to redirect her ocular sockets in an effort to salvage what remained of her focus.

Returning to the tedious calculations and rigid data, Opru managed several hours of productivity before her attention fell to the planet the station orbited.

It was green in hue, miasmic, a swirling cloud of noxious gas.

Or was it? That was her job to discover, as it was Enon's just sobols before. Help was coming, but it wouldn't arrive for many more sobols.

Before this mission, the experts had evaluated her sanity, stamina, resilience. Turns out they had overestimated the results.

Opru swayed her upper limbs in succession, a tactic that once brought comfort. Now, it was merely a form of automatic gesturing, and nothing more. In the viewport the green pond planet darkened, as its solar disk withdrew to the other side. Opru longed to descend. No weighted horror was possible in the viscous hues. She would be blank, emotionless, stilled as ancient bones embedded in the strata. Suspended in whatever chemical chaos or life-altering discovery constituted its reality.

The worst was at night. The energy made the black edges of her sleeping pod breathe. An undulation of lungs threatened seizure, grasping at her own air, robbing it. This specter was a thief, she gradually understood. Stealing her nutrients, making her brittle. Removing the intricate plating of her abilities and strength. Once she finally died, she imagined her ribcage making a drum for the specter to celebrate its victory. The prospect conjured a tepid smile.

No, she realized, this heaviness of mind was unlike anything she had witnessed over the many sobols of her life. Her form mimicked concavity in response, for the energy that chewed on her seemed extra hungry, mouth agape and shadowed. It ducked into corners where steps never needed to venture, where ocular sockets never directly observed.

And when she fell to the ground and laid there, unable to do anything at all, the weight lowered itself over her, a shroud of resignation.

Of course, she didn't belong on the floor, sniffling and vacant. Sentient beings were expected to be upright, to demonstrate their dissimilarities to less refined creatures. Her wildness would only tear off the sheet to expose their own innate proclivities and force them to *see*. Some on her homeworld believed they were evolved beyond these tendencies. But she would show them the truth if ever she returned.

All it took was a mind that corroded itself, finding the villain within.

There was no delineation between her thoughts and the vicious background babble of the station. Its voice was tinged amber and melodious as honey. If she listened, it would pour into the shell of her auditory feature. It wasn't sticky nor pungent. Nevertheless, she could taste it.

Unlike those depressions that visited in the past, tempting her to oblivion, this current energy summoned a specific madness of the soul, more insidious. Barren as an old structure long surrendered for vines, stringy biologics that layered broken walls, and shuddering every time the wind deployed, it eased into her. An exoskeleton revealing an elapsed existence, where reality was forced to crack at the pressure. She harbored these truths in her jagged palms.

Uncountable sobols passed, unblinking, and she eroded as she awaited help. Her communications were close to nonexistent, and her employers grew concerned. They said they were hurrying. They inquired what she had done with Enon's remains, but she did not explain.

In isolation, anguish set its harmony, struck resonant, making her smallest materials vibrate inside her.

Soon, the green below called again, loud as the vacancy of space, and she answered. Under two of the moons—one seemingly crouched, the other oddly expectant—she left the confines of the station, veering toward the planet below. She tracked the sinuous upper atmosphere and planned where she would enter. The shuttle would only survive such a distance for so long.

A light colored on the control panel, bright and warning.

Opru ignored it in favor of the more viscerally immediate.

There was no turning back. Her chemicals were boiled and brewed into an unprecedented concoction, steeped and assembled and made unnatural. Sorrow-filled and empty as it etched out its home.

With autopilot engaged, Opru descended, utterly still inside the small oval ship. A string seemed to tug her closer, hypnotizing and erasing in equal measure. The approach exceeded time or the confines of it, and she merely stared.

At last, she would meet her tormentor.

On the brim of this world, close to eclipse and discontinuity, she hovered. The subtle corruption embraced her, a final relenting she had sworn never to plummet inside. This was a nuisance of simplicity and inevitability too grotesque to have looked at directly: the battle of the mind against itself.

Hanging at the precipice, she spread her arms and howled her farewell.

Accepting the sounds with whispery wet replies, the planet's gasses amassed a strange, countering consensus.

She heard the murmur of the deep and inhaled sharply. Her private specter had swayed at the periphery in shades of grey and black for many sobols. But by her invitation, it uncloaked and released an enveloping radiance, shedding a glow both viscous and gilt. Dappled upon the atmospheric clouds, she watched the soft undulation and leaned toward it, shuttle tilting forward. Here, she was welcome. Doom was not but a choice.

It loomed ahead of her, and having already taken Enon, the energy lapped impatiently at her.

Too impatient. Too ugly in its covetousness. She tumbled backward in the ship.

Her mouth was dry, torso and extremities cloyingly damp. But a burgeoning desperation outweighed her resignation.

She wanted to live.

Her upper limbs bent like jagged branches and grasped the controls, slicing into the furthest layers of mysterious green, and for a moment she could swear she heard an echoing howl. She reengaged autopilot and returned to the station, a prison or sanctuary, but one she welcomed. As she removed the space suit, such an unnecessary thing considering what she had planned to do, a smear of black materialized beyond the ship. The grim presence seemed to observe her regretfully.

I want to live, she said aloud. *You may never leave me. You may persist for all my future days. But so will I.*

She stood and settled her limbs in the most comforting arrangement, watching the planet still. Later, she deemed it merely a hallucination. But in the moment, the corporeal revenant startled and diminished in size. And as she returned to life on the station, her haunting followed behind. A perpetual voyeur, but one whose power had been rescinded.

Wavelength

The star speaks on streaks of light.

Concentric and unyielding, sent out like sparks and protests, flashes of rebellion unobserved.

This one is a spheroid dusted in higher spectrum hues, mid-sized compared to the nearest compatriots, and nearing middle age. The core churns out what is needed to speak, to release its messages, requirements for more than survival. And the objective is clear as arching plasma against the black backdrop of space: find another.

Thin as gossamer and stretched beyond breaking—a bright thread pulled from the star's interior—it slips onward. Words fragile and yearning hover on the wavelength, riding the line until it reaches the auditory and visual receptors of some unfortunate being.

This light speak traverses distances that encompass the whole, a darkness expanding without end. Within the empty sea-void murmurs and shrieks travel, hurdles few yet profound. The star seeks to fill it up, give weight to the volume, give mass to the silence.

The star sings of initiation with the most sparks. A prism of its birth of collision and chemical compression, the result a cascade of color more expansive than matter. And yet, even the vibrations of illumination can be turned solid, changed and contorted when forced into the process. Still louder, the star calls out, knowing its inevitable collapse, its lifespan too long and too short simultaneously. The notes hold regret for such isolation and grief for its sentence.

Something new draws near, elongated and reflective, and it pauses close to the star. Its rotation is the only change, and the star wonders of its purpose. With renewed fervor, the star shoots out its soliloquy and hopes it is captured, understood. Why else would it be here but to make contact?

Finally, a speck departs the solid mass, tethered by the thinnest thread the star can imagine. It is not strong. It is not wise. But the star does not understand all things, a truth that was accepted in its early years. Perhaps this is the response it has craved.

Thus, the star finds its witness, at last, and catches them in the curvature of luminance. This one will suffice, the star believes, committing to fully use each precious moment of the being's brief lifespan.

The being is so small, swathed in metal and silicone, vulnerable to all the cacophonous silence surrounding them. There are no signs that anyone attends it, and the star wonders. The star grips the shape in a wide beam and suspends it aloft, tendrils of its body splayed around.

"You will listen," the star sparkles. "You will understand."

Starwords form as warm beams and everything releases at once. There is relief in the letting go, the expression. The star continues its usual rotational shifting and yet does so much more; that of connecting.

Messages in the brilliance burn the being's mind. It protests at first, shrieking against the onslaught, a curious mind that merely sought awareness of the star's unique phenomena. Or so the star guesses. There is a twinge of sorrow at this realization. Each one extending itself toward the other, only to meet in the space between and find the clarity of failure.

The star persists.

Soon, the being fills with awareness until the constraints are met, pressed outward, exceeded. The star releases what it considers an apology, softer light, less brittle, less stark. But it is too late, and the being goes motionless, the tether all that shifts as starlight bathes the vicinity.

The star stops all light-speak, dimming dangerously and immediately. Perhaps the little being needs rest. The star acquiesces, keeps itself quiet and dark for longer than it should.

The being does not stir. The capsule nearby does not leave.

Such violence is new to the star, for never has it deliberately wounded another. It has never observed how its fierce compounds and lacerating radiation have disrupted the space Beyond the discernible. This transgression brings shame in multitudes.

To the star's horror, the small being remains for a grueling period of time, a monumental mistake and a chain of remembrance.

That is until another capsule arrives and hovers by the first. The star knows more little beings move inside it, though it dare not speak again. The newcomers retrieve the being floating in space, though the star doesn't know precisely why. Perhaps to recognize the passing of life. Or to study the circumstances.

The star does not let itself consider how its information may be harvested.

Soon, there are bright flashes from the second transportation capsule. The star ignores, bereft. Strangely, the flashes continue, and the star wonders.

Do they crave to hear me?

How do they know?

Should I try again?

More transportation capsules strike through space and enshroud the star. It does not understand, and it fears the outcome.

Flashes all around become the norm, and steady beams rotate its sphere. Finally, with reluctance, the star begins to speak once more, light ribboning from the center, startling white sections allocated for each ship.

And the capsules create a responding symphony, a circle of conversation. It takes time and then the star comprehends, hears, *feels* the stories known and stories born all amongst the gases.

Eventide

Time is a construct without tangible meaning on a planet locked in rotation around a star.

This is a place of enduring contrast—acutely bifurcated—where one half sees perpetual daylight and the other constant night.

Half burns under a sun with unwavering persistence, so pristine it nearly drips through the fingers. The second hemisphere basks in a shadow thick enough to pool on the ground and cling to every form. The disparity of these is jagged, mimicked by the lives of its varying societies. Living apart, the divided domains do not interact unless they must.

Sahir notes the chime of a new hour and loosens her shirt, its white fabric ricocheting the artificial illumination from overhead. She manages composure as she considers what comes next. It is a trip she has taken many times already. Still, nerves fray with the intention.

Simultaneously, and not so far-flung, Nakil's attention catches on the droning announcement of her completed shift. Weariness splinters her joints but she hurries, understanding with discomfort how finite the opportunity.

Creeping through the Glare demands stealth, camouflage, and bribes. Nakil is an expert in such things. She can manage all of that without issue, with sufficient time.

Once more, the word proves inadequate. But she cannot

tarry on the philosophical, the intangible concept of the indefinite passage of seconds, measured by necessity rather than natural phenomena; the protracted trickle of it, whether the sun moves from its zenith at all.

To traverse the Murk warrants less skill for Sahir. She swaths herself in the blackest clothes and picks her way through the buildings, evading anyone meandering their city.

If they notice her, which has occurred, they do not approach. Despite her attempts at disguise, they sense her power, her significance, no matter how little she craves either. Such things are undefined within the self but made real by negative space, that carved out concept of *legacy*. She would rather construct identity without lineage or inheritance, but the objective proves challenging.

Of course, descending from those who have ruled the Murk for generations gives Sahir an edge, one to peer over and glimpse the forbidden side that light drenches. Her heart lurches toward the brightest of all, unrivaled in that shimmery plane of existence. She would defy more than social and political demands to wrap Nakil in her arms.

For her journey, Nakil casts herself in a shroud of off-yellow, a background hue in her illuminated realm from which attention ripples off of. Her attire includes a hood that drapes her face, hiding the pale hair she keeps short. Anticipation strings her muscles tense.

She steals through the sector she reluctantly calls home, putrid with its everlasting effulgence, yearning for the forgiving twilight and its reprieve from eye-shattering incandescence. But most of all, she seeks the comfort of Sahir's frame, the strength of her body.

Nakil draws closer, skirting the awareness of those would who would be scandalized by the intended liaison. They continue with their duties, tasks. There are many about, and she swallows a gulp of her canteen, willing herself lucky.

Between the extremes, the delineation forms, a setting where night meets morning and in reverse, where no one can count on hours slipping away. It is paused, but not in a harrowing way. Rather, it endures, a vow of early blush on the clouds and final dappled farewell.

Upon the curve of subdued dusk, Nakil sees her, black clothes melting into the tones of night. She emerges from the aching reach of daylight, sighing into the cool folds of the gloaming. Upon the binary world, within a band of determined mingling, the two come together.

Sahir raises her arms, pleading for her innate fire. Nakil sprints the last stretch, casting herself into Sahir's tide of evening. They are carried, a symmetry struck resonant on the terminus rim.

They murmur the other's name.

And next their lips join, a rush of flesh seeking depth. The connection reaches further, limbs tightening as space thins around their shared crepuscule sky.

It is impermissible by both their governments to exist on this middle ribbon of flowing equilibrium. Those who rule the sundered globe have agreed it is prohibited. To be found here would warrant nothing but swift death for the inconsequential Nakil. Punishment would be less harsh for Sahir, but losing Nakil would yield more profound wounds than anything Sahir's disappointed family could inflict.

They shudder, clothes banished in favor of skin and pigment from the invariably bruised pink and crushed peach colors scattered around them. Moans follow the trees, which sway in the benign wind, limbs bowing against the backdrop of nighttime vespers or daytime dimness.

"I want to give you the shade you seek," Sahir says when their forms have come to stillness.

Nakil listens, tremulous and believing, resting in Sahir's

arms. "You deserve the light, too."

Sahir pulls Nakil closer, skin clammy from their exertion. "I know nothing but the Murk. That is where I belong."

"And you think I belong in the Glare? Where nothing is hidden? All on display? No," Nakil says, more firmly than she intended. "I want this. Where I can have both the supposed exquisite and the profane."

Sahir chuckles, the exhale sweeping her bare torso and leaving goosebumps. She runs her fingers over Nakil's collarbone, indulging the desire to conjure a similar reaction. She is rewarded with a quirked grin, and Nakil raises a hand to her sweaty locks, which ease around the searching knuckles.

"The Murk is too morbid. You would tire of it quickly."

Nakil sits up, forehead compressing. "Do you mean I will tire of you?"

Lips tight, Sahir rocks to her knees and gazes across the amaranthine landscape. Absently, she retrieves her shirt from the ground. Nakil glowers at the lack of response.

"You're wrong. I want to be with you, no matter the consequences."

Sahir meets her eyes, tenderness making her jaw go slack. For a moment, she fears the onset of sorrow, a profoundly unwelcome sensation in Nakil's warm presence.

Forgoing words, Sahir embraces her, mouth dipping to hers.

"May I be your eternal shadow, then? Distanced, but not severed."

Nakil's grief hitches, a flash of uncertainty making her squint. But she nods, kissing Sahir through the motion, tears mingling with their sweat.

"Yes. But not as something I create, not an absence. You are something that exists in connection with me. And for that, I am grateful."

24

Her insistence makes Sahir's eyes sting. Grasping tight, they abandon reality and its constraints. Nakil rolls them over, spurred by Sahir's eager, deep-belly undertones. Her hands run the length of Nakil's body, both yielding and appetent. Their lids shutter, ushering forth a velvet maroon shade where they alone exist.

In sequence they eclipse, passion rustling the vegetation that rings their clearing. Nakil collapses, chest to chest heaving. At last, she speaks a muttering confession.

"I love you, my deepening nightfall."

"And I love you, my rising aurora."

Sahir's words and heartbeat thud against Nakil's ribcage, a mimicking rhythm, and she smiles softly.

In their union, sun and shade collect, early and late amass. High noon and midnight lose antipodal variance, an unexpected reforging of a balance long relinquished, long mourned.

First Contact

Strata part for us, descending at speed and force. True surface perceived and witnessed. Large splendor everywhere. Asom All fill with hope. We arrive of buoyant energy and resolute thought. Gulin at last. We find our place.

The aquiline ship dipped into the atmosphere like the sacred aberith fish in its ancestral sea, as light yellow layers of cloud-matter and foliage detritus flit away from the curved silver-hued sides. Menageries floated around them, aloft, and strung together via thick, gnarled root bridges, covered in specimens of various saturated pigments. Their sensors gathered sounds of wildlife interacting on each one, weather buffeting around them, followed by a disquieting high-pitched song from an unidentified source.

To its frustration, Asom Three couldn't define any explanation for such colorful masses levitating against the known laws of nature. It saw long tendrils of vines growing off the edges of one, tall rock columns punctuating the surface of another, and impossible amounts of water gurgling from the center of one. Creatures of various shapes and heights leapt above the miniature landscape, hunting, hiding. As Asom Three watched, it felt relief that none of the creatures went over the edge to their likely deaths.

There was much to understand about such improbabilities, yet that would come later. Asom All nudged the curious Asom Three on to the next question; a location to land.

Asom Six, tonal quality brightening with satisfaction, alerted them to a safe position atop an extensive plain, near a dramatic canyon filled with deep, tactile colors.

Asom Two swirled the sensors, eliciting saccharine beeps throughout their station, while Asom Five diligently checked in with the crew members dispersed throughout the oblong vessel. The other Asoms inhabiting the bridge searched for signs of intelligent life, hope—one of their primary biological motivations—discernible in each large eye. Research from a distance could only reveal so much. Already they were learning much more.

Asom All of Past identified this planet, orange-hued and spheroid, dangling as one does over an endless expanse. They deemed it suitable, rich in mineral, flush with potential. As their planet deteriorated following increasingly heightened radiation from their dying star, the Asom searched for many uhlras. And more uhlras were spent traveling to Gulin, one of the few planets seemingly suitable.

As is custom, Asom Two, Three, and Five approach on flow foot, and it descends like weight. Here, firm reassurance guides All, and All follow in same line of movement. We hope to find the first, the ones who preexist Asom All.

The Asom navigated the planet's terrain for some time, sensors emitting a ceaseless range of colors and readings. Fatigue encroached as they surveyed the high hills and peered into the darkened valleys. Much attention was devoted to the perusal of organic life, which looked like dried tendrils to the Asom. They discovered small legged beings with irregular spikes, plants that curled into themselves in reaction to loud noises, and holes in the ground wherein luminous plumes seemed to track them.

Above, the menageries dangled effortlessly, casting a shifting pattern of shadows. Asom Two scanned each impossible mass they passed beneath, its shadow making them contract from the change in temperature, and discovered discrete biomes upon them. Asom Two could not yet extrapolate anything, and remained focused on the singular task of remedying that.

Soon, worry wove through the Asom as the sky gradually blackened. The prospect of hidden dangers made its consciousness tremble. Two, Three, and Five conjoined, and considered returning to the ship to rest until the next star cycle. Then a new sound reached them, florid and layered, increasing in volume as time elapsed.

Uncertainty formed in the All Thought, but Asom Five dictated for the living document.

As is custom, Asom Two, Three, and Five stand in place as one, while beings of unknown origin approach. Sensor shows many in number and the ground trembles. Fear creeps up, vile, then Asom on ship send whispercares in droves. We glean the hope. We are resolute as Gulin itself. Asom seek serenity amongst the unfamiliar. Send whispercares to our home Asoms.

Over the crest in the eastern quadrant of Gulin rode a group of native inhabitants, ribbons adorning their apparent organic carriers as they hurtled their approach. There was nothing else to discern until they drew closer.

Then, it was too late for reversal, and the Asom whole hummed with the amassed intention this was not their end.

The Asom ship slipped lower in the sky. The inhabitants reached them. On the surface, the Unified Three Asom extended their palms in customary greeting and waited for first contact.

Inhale

Frederick approaches the windows in the living room, his movements stilted, controlled.

He tears away the layer of thick plastic, taped and stapled over the boarded frames he once adored. The natural light was one of the reasons he wanted to buy this house.

With an impatient tug on a resistant staple, he rips the plastic layer and tosses it aside. *Gabe would scold me for throwing trash on the floor. He would scold me more for what I'm about to do.*

He positions the drill, eyes on the line of screws keeping the two-by-fours in place—the ones initially intended to become a backyard porch—and readies himself to eliminate what separates him from the outside world.

Their plans for the porch hadn't been extravagant; a nice sitting area, a grill, some outdoor pillows for pops of color. None of that mattered now. The yard sat empty save for a few rectangular raised beds, the vegetable starters withered from lack of water.

The two of them had thought their attempts at boarding, taping, and covering every crevice with plastic would be adequate to keep out the toxin. But that was the kind of folly that excavates the throat, mauls the heart. The arrogance that they were different. That they would somehow survive.

I'm sorry.

There's a distant, choking sob that erupts. Frederick realizes it originated in his chest, his clenched esophagus. Already he's a ghost, taking up space left vacant. With his face swollen from crying, he wrenches the screws out one by one.

The drill was a Christmas present from Gabe, of course. It was on sale, his beloved had insisted, knowing that Fred would protest a costly gift just after purchasing a house. Not that the house was fancy. It needed a lot of work, and they had planned to do it all themselves.

"We can't own a house without a set of tools. And I know how much you miss working on things with your dad," Gabe had said. The look Gabe had given him was tender and Fred could only meet his gaze, forcing back the sting of tears.

There was so much more I meant to build. So much more we wanted to do.

Gabe died four hours ago. He wasn't supposed to. Anyone else could have died, and did, but not Gabe. He was solid, rooted, a rock that Fred could cling to as the waves of existence drowned everything else.

Fred blinks hard, sucks in another breath, clenches his fists. He feels like a child. All he can keep thinking is *this isn't fair. Nothing about this is fucking fair.*

He keeps working, the whine of the power tool a shrill soundtrack. At last, the final board comes loose, plummeting to the floor and hitting Fred's toe. He hadn't looked down, hadn't paid attention. *Oh well. What's a sore toe on the brink of extinction?* He grits his teeth against the pain.

He knows that his air is no longer pure. The infiltration is global, ravaging the world without concern, leaving a few people scattered across continents, or so the last broadcast hypothesized. Who could know for sure? Surprisingly, the electricity lasted longer than anything else.

The toxin has now killed every person Fred has ever met, every person who poured joy or sadness or rage or malaise into his thirty-three years of life.

But in the hollowed out quiet of his home, only a single person's death matters on this silent Thursday morning. A single individual who left him behind, who painted the walls of this house in crooked overalls. One person who had convinced Fred to cultivate hope.

Wind whispers, squeezing through the infinitesimal gaps of the glass panes, smeared with the fingerprints of his dead husband. He chooses not to notice.

His perception grows fuzzy, unfocused on what the present moment offers. He lingers on the salty sting of what came before. Even the last days, marred by protracted dread and horror, were warmed by the fact that they weren't alone; monitoring the decay of society, preparing and eating meals, thinking of the people dying in mass, horrific unison.

Eventually, Fred observes the rushing resonance that signals the start of it.

The end of it, he corrects inwardly. Gabe's voice arrives, a recollection stirred: "For if there's anything that's always true about Frederick, it's that he's a pragmatist," he'd once said.

Fred almost smiles at the sensation of Gabe's voice reverberating across a crowded room, a memory that feels so far away as to be something Fred made up. A time when having people over to show off your new home was logical. When loving a person unabashedly was the most important thing following years of rejection and disappointment.

That last point is still true, at least.

He sways, thoughts turning nondescript and delicate, each one popping under too much scrutiny.

The toxin continues to overrun his system. He imagines it

skipping along his neurons, laying waste to the subtle marvelous wonders of his body. Ripping even the memory of Gabe from him.

The pair had been warriors, but out of necessity, not choice. They'd fought for every piece of their shared life, losing family and friends in the process. The realization that all of the people who rejected them are dead is concave.

Gabe is dead, he reminds himself. But Gabe is near, still. Or what remains of him.

We sure showed them, huh? Didn't we show them all?

Fred moves backward, tripping on a chair and colliding with the corner of the coffee table. He yelps, but there is no impulse to cushion the impact. He simply falls.

Laying prostrate, he glances warily at his hands, a brown that combines the onyx and bronze of his parents. Fred clamps his eyes shut. For years, he had hoped to have a child whose skin blended his own and Gabe's. Someone to raise feeling strong and beautiful in their body, which society deemed less than. Gabe was on board. Always *onboard*.

But the timing had been wrong. They needed to finish grad school. They needed to buy a house. Last, they had brainstormed how to convince the adoption agency that an interracial gay couple with limited savings would be able to pull off raising a child. Each one seemed like a frail excuse now.

A sob ravages his torso. The sound doesn't make it all the way out, lodging in the cavern around his heart. He emits another stilted choke and curls into a ball. Panic corrodes him until he thinks of Gabe—alive, vibrant, his.

He breathes deeply, partially in resignation, partially out of habit. It was something Gabe made him practice over and over to reach a mindful state. *Even here, at the edge of all things, he manages to comfort me. Even if breathing is the very thing that invites my death.*

His lungs begin to protest, unwilling to fully inflate.

Contaminated. That was the word everyone used just eight days ago. Now, his whole house, his body is contaminated. The level of invasion makes his stomach churn.

"You're pathetic." The words drip cynicism yet he has to stop himself from laughing.

Gabe's body isn't even cold and already you're killing yourself. No surprise there. But I never tried to surprise anybody. Just tried to figure it all out.

A green haze blankets everything. The particles rush through his mouth, sharp and vicious. He doesn't feel that. The next part is what's excruciating; they pour into his esophagus and adhere to the intricate crevices of his lungs. The scourge presses harder, acute and ruthless. His brain seizes on an unrelenting thought: *I can't escape this.*

But where the hell would I go?

He wrenches into a seated position. When the initial cough arrives, spurred by his rush of movement, phlegm pools in his hand, thick bodily fluids not meant to be seen. Fred flinches and swipes his hand against the old flannel shirt. One of Gabe's. Blue and black.

Wearing it makes it seem like Gabe is just out of sight.

Fred's heart compresses, the spores infesting that vital organ. His pulse turns erratic. *Didn't you know, Gabe? My body can't seem to function without you. You are the reason for it all. And you're gone.*

Gabe, with his smiling oval eyes and quirked lips. His scrappy mustache that wouldn't grow beyond the corners of his mouth. His pursed expression when grading papers, bent over, reading every word his students assembled and turned in.

Fred exhales, but it's wholly different. More of a jagged spurt, signaling a demise, an ending. He'd heard Gabe make the same wet rasp before stilling entirely.

In the deepening sludge of his consciousness, Fred visualizes placing his fingers on either side of his love's face, Gabe's honeyed-auburn skin warm, the hint of wrinkles just beginning. There was so much to love about that man. And somehow, Gabe loved Fred, too.

A baffling thing. A wondrous thing. Burning bright until the very brink.

Dawn light struck Gabe's face the best. A fresh glimmer that set eyelashes ablaze and freckles to glowing spots. Now, shadows pooled around his form, contents of a bag spilled around him. The toxin had found its way into the gas mask Gabe had worn to the abandoned grocery store. A tiny, undetectable leak. Something they missed. Something that slowly destroyed what was left.

Fred had begged him not to go. They still had food, though not much. They needed to limit risk. But Gabe had been so sure it was better to be prepared.

Their mask wasn't top of the line; it was only part of a Halloween costume. Gabe shrugged, claiming it was a high-end costume store, promising to come back. That they couldn't stay inside indefinitely.

But the world had started flaking apart with exquisite precision. Faster than it should have, making it obscenely clear it was simply removing the weight of humanity.

Frederick grimaces, considering what his spouse said when first he heard this musing. "You're personifying nature. It wasn't a decision made by the earth," Gabe argued the third night in isolation. "Only an unfortunate inevitability when given sufficient time."

There's a fight in his lungs and his teeth grind. *Fuck this. Battlefields should never be invisible.*

He thinks of the fields where he gathered fireflies as a child. How his sister Lucy preferred to catch toads, bulbous and croaking their disdain.

He recalls the waterfall that Gabe described with such

37

affection, nostalgia etching his features. Gabe had taken him there on their honeymoon. They skinny-dipped under a crescent moon.

"Will we ever stop taking the world for granted?" Gabe had asked as he laced his hand with Fred's in the water. They had to work at it because their fingers never fit quite right.

"With you, I don't take anything for granted," Fred had said, bringing their hands to his lips.

Fred screams himself hoarse, fingernails digging canals into the wood floor. *We couldn't decide on this floor for so long. This was the compromise. This wood was our compromise.*

Breathing becomes a chore of dedication and focus. To inhale, he pushes his chest. A stickiness of tissue resists his efforts. Then he pulls in air infested with dangerous particles he couldn't explain if his life depended on it. The process is a struggle, his body protesting the violation as long as it can.

Was it not worth the joy of our love? Was the act of our rebellion not enough? I thought it would have been enough.

There's a brazen impulse to crawl to the kitchen, to expire beside Gabe. But his energy has left with dazzling speed. The air is quicksand, sucking him into its void, its soundlessness.

A shudder unravels him, startling a groan from his ravaged form. It hurts. Everything hurts.

But then, lightness replaces all else. Without warning, the feeling of his body calcifying and disintegrating ceases. Without warning, it feels as though everything is normal again and then marvelous.

He becomes an unbound thing, uplifted and released. The sensation makes him sigh.

His mind manufactures a final grip of cognizance: *Is this what dying feels like? Or is it a gift of the toxin to remove us through effervescence?*

Gabe had always been fond of poetry, and his enthusiasm had

gradually influenced Fred, like drops of ink released into still water.

Fred glances around, lips parted and eyes wide, his breath suspended. They had been so proud of this house. It would have been the best gathering place on the block.

His head hits the floor with a dull thud. The wood grain presses into his cheek, tiny narrow veins of a tree that once lived. He lays in silence and surrender, fingers clutching his wedding ring.

Between Boughs

Employee 12, is it time for your scheduled Therapy.
Please leave your work station in clean order, and
proceed to Unit 2 on your floor. Thank you for your
dedication, and please enjoy your Session.

Therapy breaks are mandatory. They are scheduled once a
week for each employee. You cannot tell how many employees there
are beyond your floor, and have little sense of how many floors there
are. None of that is relevant, and therefore, you do not think of it.

This office building is designed to incorporate extensive
natural light. It enters the structure from the highest level and is
mirrored, bounced, and refracted downward. Further, the physical
environment is all white, as are the employee uniforms, and research
conducted by the Company highlight the vital need for breaks in
Nature.

You look forward to this Session every week. An
announcement arrived this morning that multiple changes to the
Therapy Units were implemented and tested recently. This will be
your first experience with the advancements. You try to hide your
enthusiasm.

The three Units stand on the eastern edge of the floor, in a
straight line. They are identical, shining, and hide a great wonder

inside. If one was to look only at the exterior and watch people venture inside for up to two hours, the observer might feel confusion about what occurs therein.

You have a spring in your step.

With a practiced ease, your employee badge passes over the identification pad, and the Unit chirps, as if happy with your arrival. You can't hide your smile now.

You enter through the sliding door, and leave the office, the Company, and Reality behind you.

You ease inside the bright white cylinder, fingers warming on the soft surface. Once you have shut the door, the green light on the exterior shifts to a gentle red; not a shade of anger, but a "Please wait until this Therapy Unit is available," hue. That is how your colleagues read the red light. An understanding without words.

Now, there is no more noise of productivity, machines, and connection. The colleagues who occupy this floor with you no longer need to exist in your mind. With abandon, you relax and allow the sounds of Nature to submerge you.

Your body settles onto the cushion while your mind decides you are walking inside a forest.

Welcome, Employee 12. You are a vital member of this Company. Without your efforts, this Company would fail to reach its goals. Thank you for your commitment and professionalism, Employee 12. Over the past six months, you have achieved several promotions and according to our records, you will receive another soon if your work continues to exceed expectation. Enjoy your Therapy Session, Employee 12. Enjoy Nature.

The automated voice goes silent. For a moment, you wonder why the Unit has not designated how long your session will last. But this does not trouble you for more than a second.

The immersion begins and you walk into a forest beneath a blue sky.

Ground covered in short grasses and fuzzy mosses appears beneath your feet. You never counter this response—you bend over and brush the surfaces with your fingertips. Above, a flock of birds coast by, so effortlessly weightless that their wings need not move at all. Around you, trees press close, the bark rivulets of texture and smells. Colors appear, vibrant and varied, across the forest.

Wind glides around the trunks, catching the blue cuffs of your sleeves, now the permitted casual attire of Therapy. Your bare feet sink ever so slightly into the dewy ground and the layers of organic detritus. Warm sunlight slants through the boughs, and your head rolls backward, base of skull resting on top of spinal cord. Your mouth falls open, an inhale commences, and you stand utterly still in the thick beam of light.

If only this could happen more than once a week. In fact, you would love to live here forever.

You think briefly of the rumor that the higher an employee climbs at the Company, the longer that employee gets to spend in the Therapy Unit. Perhaps this does not make sense, since the Company must succeed and each employee is necessary to achieve those goals, but it is motivating, at least.

A sparkle on the horizon draws your eyes. You know what it is already, have spent much of your Sessions in those clear, cold waters. Sometimes you dip only your toes. Sometimes you fully submerge.

There is nothing else like it in Reality.

Therapy is only a professional perk for those who work at your Company, and you are proud of all you have accomplished to have earned your place. This is a gift from your employer, to know the giddy delight of sun, to dunk in a lake, to pluck berries from a bush and taste them.

No, you would never do anything to jeopardize your place at this Company. You know there are thousands of people in Reality who crave a place here, just right *here*, for the sensory gift of Nature. Though your body merely sits in the Unit, your mind, heart, and soul soar freely.

You feel a sudden urge to drink, and the Unit you inhabit understands. A glass materializes in the air, hovering by your left hand. The liquid smells like lemons. You drink it at once.

Then you imagine a blanket would be nice to relax on, under the shade of the trees, with the lake at your feet. In response, a rectangular swath of fabric stretches out beside you on the ground. You lay upon it eagerly. Distant thoughts of returning to work materialize, of all the tasks you must accomplish during the work round, and you remind yourself not to stay too long.

The Unit will alert you when your Session has expired, of course. You decide not to worry. Worrying is the opposite of what this place is for.

These are excellent updates they have programmed into Therapy, you think. Your eyes shut, and the gentle waves on the shore shape a profound serenity into which you fit perfectly. Your last desire is to never leave, to never exit and return to Reality. This desire is impossible. You smile nonetheless.

Sleep claims you, and you succumb.

———————

Employee 77, please observe the red light. Employee

12 currently occupies this Therapy Unit. You should have been notified that your scheduled Session was shifted to Unit 3. Please proceed to your scheduled Session.

Employee 77 squints briefly. Employee 77 remembers noting that Employee 12 entered this Unit two days prior, and intended to ask how the updates seemed after the Session. It is impossible that Employee 12 remains inside the Unit. Perhaps the Unit is malfunctioning, for the rules state clearly that no one may remain in the Unit for more than two hours. Despite the confusion, Employee 77 follows instructions and enters Unit 3.

After all, Therapy is mandated by the Company. Employee 77 would hate to have a note of insubordination added to their file because of a Unit's malfunction.

Immersion begins at once, and Employee 77 walks into a forest beneath a blue sky.

Collapse on a Distant Mental Landscape

It named itself in dreams.

Marin rolled over in bed, body twitching to the reverberations in her mind, and her leg straightened convulsively. Sonny whined at the inadvertent kick, but nestled closer to Marin, wet nose tucked under a paw. Within seconds, the dog snored again.

The human's eyelids scrunched like a rug caught under a couch. Her teeth clacked, a brittle sound in the semi-quiet of the city's night, a mimicking of the ceiling fan above.

She wanted to wake the hell up.

In the cloister of her dream, Marin stood atop a hill, eyes stuck to an orb that floated a hundred feet above. It dangled illogically, still and serene, its surface gleaming like wet metal. And yet it was more than that. The swirls of iridescence, so reminiscent of a bubble, moved across the great curved plain, taking up a huge swath of the sky. As the electrified pinks, purples, blues, and greens tangled and spun, so too did Marin's interior, as if she were a puppet on play by this massive, crushing abnormality. As the dream wore on, the rumblings disassembled her slowly, her parts dissolving into nothing more than black filings shaken in an Etch-a-Sketch.

She labeled this a bad dream, but struggled to end it.

Since childhood, Marin had claimed lucidity in her dreams, yet this was a different challenge. Less of her own mental landscape where she might explore and create, this gave the impression of a prison. And the jailer was a smear overhead, hovering and murmuring and conjuring a seeming madness.

Indecipherable words flowed through the experience. She squinted, focused all of her energy on listening, slicing through the conflicting sounds until she grasped the words. The answer was no comfort, however, as the phrase on repeat seemed to pick her up off the ground to carry her skyward.

On the fold. On the fold. On the—

This needed to end.

Dream Marin forced her mouth open to scream, releasing such volume it struck the miasma above her visually, rattling it backward into the upper layers of atmosphere. Then she transformed its surface, with skill honed over two decades of lucid self-training, into a massive clock. The hour hand struck, and a shriek erupted, blasting her onto the ground.

Finally awake, she shot upright, panting, and nearly knocked Sonny to the floor.

"Fuck," she said, breath a shallow ferocity, her hand pressed to her chest.

Clammy and shaking, she slipped out of bed and walked to the bathroom, but no amount of splashing water helped. The cold only made the muscles of her face ache.

She returned to her fluffy covers and excess of pillows, but dreaded sleep.

"Come here, cutie," she said quietly. Sonny joined her and she scratched under his chin. "That was terrible."

She didn't want to look at the actual clock.

A yawn escaped, and she rubbed her eyes. "What was that

thing saying? I can't even remember now."

Sonny lifted his head toward her.

She ruffled the hair between his ears—a spout of wiry white—and tried to untangle her thoughts. Something about a fold, she decided. It had repeated over and over in the nightmare until she feared it would never leave her. Now it seemed too distant to hold meaning.

Marin relented and read the clock. One thirty am. It would take her a long time to get back to sleep. She pulled her laptop from the bedside table, adorned with band stickers and national park emblems, and cracked it open. By instinct, she typed in her preferred social media site and began to scroll. This was a rote action born of prolonged habit, but she wouldn't do it all night, she promised herself. Fifteen minutes at the most.

On the right side of the screen sat the list of trending topics. Her eyes zeroed in on one in particular with such speed, it felt mechanical. The words seemed hazy on the screen, a colorful blur that wiggled if stared at too long.

She read it aloud, voice quivering. "On the fold…" She leaned forward to be sure, face mere inches from the screen. "What the hell?"

Sonny stirred, possibly concerned by her tone. He crawled closer to her arm, but she didn't notice.

Six thousand mentions of this weird phrase. No, it can't be. There's just no way.

Marin snapped her laptop closed with possibly too much force, tossed it to the other side of the bed, and buried herself under the covers.

How could one person's nightmare be trending?

She wasn't sure if she'd welcome the answer, or that it even existed. She concluded this wasn't actually happening, went to the kitchen, made a cup of slumbering tea, and brought it back to her room. It had been an excessive week, too demanding. This was only the result of exhaustion.

She crawled into the depths of her bed, pulled Sonny to her chest, and attempted to shut off her brain.

———————

Late morning forced her eyes open.

The sun seemed to have targeted her face specifically, blasting a surface area of only a few inches with such intensity as to rouse her from the stupor achieved a few hours previously. Sonny sat beside her, his narrow face insistent.

"I get it. You need breakfast," she said.

He placed both his paws together and did the yoga pose named after such dog behavior.

"I need breakfast, too." She shook herself and stood, head pulsing from the restless night, before going through the automatic steps to complete her morning checklist. It was the weekend, so she didn't have to work, but there were some client emails that required some attention.

Then the reverberation returned to her consciousness.

On the fold.

She jolted, midway to placing Sonny's bowl on the floor, and dropped it before staggering back to her room. The dog eagerly licked up the kibble scattered across the kitchen tiles.

Her tabs remained in the browser, and the number of mentions was even more baffling than when she first looked. A million. She doubted the algorithm could even track anything higher than that, and the other trending topics described different snippets of the bad dream.

Nightmare bubble cloud was accompanied by *whispering*

mirror and finally, *global nightmare* all sat in a neat column under the trending tab. The last topic, hilariously unrelated, was *soccer.*

Despite the grumble in her stomach, Marin clicked, opened new tabs, and furiously scrolled. She frowned, unable to believe the unfurling evidence.

This phenomenon seemed to have appeared in people's dreams on every continent within a single twenty-four hours.

Gaping, she watched as the numbers of shares, likes, and comments shot up, felt the panic of all these humans welling inside her. She couldn't look away, not even when Sonny rubbed her shins.

On the fold.

That's what everyone heard, an echoing voice that permeated what appeared to be every human mind on planet Earth.

How could such a thing exist, an invasion of all minds? Too many questions rose up, compounding, and after watching a handful of news clips, she quickly realized pundits had no idea what to say, and so made stuff up.

Marin rubbed her cheeks, a sudden onrush of hunger snapping her back to the present. She startled when she realized an hour had passed. Food seemed like an absurd distraction from what appeared to be a worldwide mystery, but a low disquiet in her head was motivation enough to tear her eyes away from the online spectacle.

She shoved two slices of bread into the toaster and chewed her thumbnail as they heated. Sonny sat politely by her feet, head tilted. Three quick pets and she was off again, tearing toward the medicine cabinet for Tylenol. The headache solidified, growing denser, as if it was intending to amass gravity. She winced, took several pills, and returned to her toast, slathering the slices with an excess of butter.

An idea struck her as she chewed, and she tentatively went to her front door. She peaked through the window, looking for any visible neighbors. The street was empty, and not even the apartment across the street showed signs of inhabitants.

Unease crept up her spine. There was no reason to lose rationality, no reason to be spooked. People were likely glued to their sources of news, scrolling their own feeds, texting their loves ones. Humanity was going to be fine. It had to be.

Her phone chirped a notification. She crammed the rest of her toast into her mouth—begrudging how difficult it was to chew and swallow—and grabbed the device from beside her table. She didn't have much family, and it was highly unlikely the brother she hadn't seen in ten years would be texting.

It was her boss: Marin, you okay?
Fine Kels. Just freaked out. You?
I'll also go with freaked out. Need anything?
Good, thanks.
Consider stocking up on some items… I have a bad feeling.
Marin gave a thumbs up in response.

Kels often had bad feelings, and they were always associated with astrology. Strangely, while astrology usually irked Marin, it might be at least somewhat relevant right now. After all, the human race was currently involved in a collective delusion that included a celestial object in the sky. Now it was time to figure out if and how it would affect people.

Marin grabbed her wallet, patted Sonny on the head, and left for the grocery store, assembling another list as she speed walked.

With each hurried step, dread pooled inside her like the scummy last puddle in an old pool, and she suppressed the urge to run. This took deliberate effort, rivaling the attempts to keep her breathing steady. Distantly, she noticed the air was cool, with a hint of a seasonal shift that was suddenly too far in the future to consider.

She encountered no one on her sidewalk, but she spotted a couple rushing on the opposite side of the street. Their faces were hidden behind scarfs. It wasn't that cold yet, Marin thought. *What are they hiding from?*

Fear congealed in her stomach, and she walked faster, briefly annoyed she'd forgotten her reusable shopping bag. Objectively, that was the least important issue to get hung up on. Still, it was a bummer.

She bit her lip as the store came into view. There was a mass of bodies entering and exiting, their arms either filled with overflowing bags or soon to be. She scrunched her nose.

What a fuck-up, she thought, to not come to the grocery last night. Before panic set in. Before the possibility of violence...

A window shattered nearby, and she jumped. Someone was attacking a person's car with the owner inside. The car owner slammed a foot on the gas and sped noisily away without further incident. Marin swallowed.

Joining the crowd, she elbowed to keep a small safety sphere around herself. Bread was already out, but she had some of the fancy sprouted stuff in her freezer. *It won't last long, though.* She snagged a dozen eggs, a small bag of flour, and bananas. The shelves with canned items were empty. Luckily, there were a couple of remaining jugs of water. She grabbed one, resisting the desire to take it all, and reached for several of the last toilet paper rolls.

It wasn't a great haul. But there wasn't a damn thing to do about it.

The line to check out was too long, so she withdrew her wallet and left a $50 on the counter, more than enough. The cashier, whose eyes were bloodshot, yelled once. Marin offered a regrettable expression and kept going.

She passed several more people during the return journey. One was making a low noise, a tremulous tone from deep inside their diaphragm. It reminded Marin of the nightmare. She ran the rest of the way, arms aching.

Funny how fear could be a contagious thing. Infecting them all at once. Invading their psyches, virulent and impatient.

———————

Marin didn't sleep much after that.

She found several discussion boards where people threw their wildest explanations at the virtual wall to see what would stick. She wanted to contribute her own, but hesitation formed as sweat on the nape of her neck.

Compared to her peers, she'd never felt particularly intelligent. She could whip up an architectural design in a few hours, mind quiet the whole time, but if prompted to explain something philosophical, she would feel deeply inept.

The one comment she was considering sharing to the anonymous board related to sewing, an activity she'd done with her mother as a child, long before Marin had transitioned. Parent and child had had to do engage with this activity privately, since so many would mock a child assigned a male identity at birth for engaging with sewing. Her mother had done her best, but the sense of shame was strong back then.

Now, as she finally posted her thoughts, she appreciated the unique perspective, since it proved intriguing.

One person had commented, but what does *On the Fold* mean? is it a poor translation? the name for someone? A place?

A response quickly arrived underneath. I think it's a warning.

Another said, the fuck? what's freaky. warning us about what?

The guesses poured forth. Marin typed her own. Perhaps it's instructions, like for a sewing pattern.

She wasn't sure what exactly this meant and waited for someone else to seize the concept.

wtf are you talking about?

Here it goes, she thought.

The fold is the central line in a pattern. The focal line of symmetry. You fold the fabric along that line to complete the pattern, she explained, then waited.

With fingers twined in her lap, Marin awaited judgement from these random strangers.

that's weird but interesting. but it's assuming if whatever it is has some sentience. that it knows things about humans and patterns.

Marin nodded as she read along. She was making assumptions, jumping to concepts based on her own thinking. What if that was part of the problem they were all up against? That *On the Fold* couldn't possibly be understood by them. Maybe it was entirely foreign.

Sonny nuzzled her shins, and outside her window fireworks went off. She jolted at the cacophony, distressed by the slow-motion unraveling that seemed to be occurring. The uncertainty conjured distrust, unease, and unpredictability. It was three in the afternoon on a Tuesday and people should be at work, children at school. But few were.

When another firework went off, Marin shoved away from her desk and let her laptop idle. It was enough speculating online for one day. She needed to get her mind off everything, to get her hands working, and knew just the task.

She walked into her guest room and plopped down at the sewing table. The machine felt sturdy beneath her hands, reliable, comforting. It hadn't been used in months, maybe even in a year, but it was easy to come back to.

Sonny joined at her feet, curling around the sewing machine pedal, and dozed. Marin worked through two sections of the trench coat pattern, remembering how eager she'd been to find it months ago. Still, a nagging drip of apprehension accompanied the rhythm of the machine, like a leak in the ceiling. A hole in her focus.

Several people had raised the possibility of aliens, that this was an invasion. There were always the usual theorists who contributed this explanation, no matter what the initial information was. To them, the next step after a mystery was always extraterrestrial. She used to scoff.

Now, whenever Marin came across this idea online, that a non-Earth presence was attacking them in their own minds, dread made her all clammy. She had to stand up, start pacing, and try not to bite her nails into jagged lines, a habit she had combatted since childhood.

There was no particular explanation she preferred, but chemicals in the environment building up over decades to create some toxin-related mass hallucination almost made sense. Or at least, she wanted it to.

Around the world, people grasped for *something* to make sense.

The nightmares continued for seventeen consecutive nights, and the human race—as was their nature—grew complacent, accepting the baffling new normal they shared.

Then the eighteenth night arrived.

On the Fold left the dreamscape, materializing on Planet Earth simultaneously, and this time, its presence disrupted more than online discourse and daily schedules.

Marin had slept in, and hours of updates crowded her screen, reactions and theorizing louder than any recent news. Texts from her boss Kels went unanswered. Sonny was fed because he bullied her with his barking. It was neglect, sure, of everything Marin had so recently been devoted to; her canine companion, hygiene, a social life, work.

Spaced evenly around the world like a patchwork quilt, oblong bubbles emerged across latitudes and longitudes. Each one floated half a mile in the sky, dangling without any visible power source, and unmoving.

Sonny thumped his head against Marin's shin, which hurt more than it should have. She picked him up to sit in her lap and pressed her earbuds deeper into her ears, frowning at the screen.

"They're everywhere," the reporter said. "Over the ocean. Over stadiums. Skyscrapers. Mountains. Houses. Deserts. *Everywhere.*" Her voice broke with each word, shock infused with horror lining her face. Marin shared the video to her page and clicked away on to the next post within seconds.

Fifteen minutes later, she received a text from her estranged brother, asking if she was all right, saying he and his wife and kids were fine, but scared. He said she should come stay with them, but he used her deadname. She didn't respond, still hearing his vitriol the last time they spoke.

For hours, she barely breathed, lips chapping as she devoured whatever she could find online. Much of it was fear mongering; spiritualists claiming they were portals to a higher dimension, ready to ascend anyone who had worked through past life karma. Others said it was a collapse of the multiverse and soon reality would break. Another faction claimed it was Jesus Himself.

The President of the United States gave an update on how seriously the government was taking the development, not yet classifying it as a dire threat, but working to understand what was transpiring without delay. Celebrities filmed themselves freaking out in their luxurious homes, while survivalists outlined what they recommended stockpiling before the inevitable. It was a vague term used over and over, the *inevitable.*

Air travel was canceled globally. What if an airplane flew into one? Would flying near it trigger a response? Did the laws of physics remain the same surrounding the phenomena? Marin wasn't a scientist, but with a well of morbid fixation, she found every possible expert speaking on the matter.

It was late afternoon by the time she decided to go outside.

Marin didn't have to walk far to find her closest *On the Fold*. Plus, she'd discovered a map of each one's location. There were 2,684 in total, a very specific number with no obvious significance.

She was finally ready to witness it for herself. The reality, too displaced via a screen, demanded the immediacy of direct observation. Like the ability to guide her own dreams, she rallied her focus and stepped outside.

The sun would set soon, and the opalescent curve in the sky reflected the light coldly, as if the hue was seeped of warmth. Marin navigated between neighbors, strangers, gawkers, and worshippers. Dozens of chairs and blankets dotted a grassy. People sat beneath the structure, discussing, drinking, debating. Some held signs, but Marin ignored them, already guessing that they rambled about God or some other supreme being or aliens or the most recent billionaire who had flown into space.

Her eyes swept the oval, a ripple in the sky like watercolor armor, mirroring but distorting the light. She walked carelessly through the camped out crowd, the stares and comments barely registering.

"The first you're seeing it? Where've you been?" a man said, snorting a laugh at her.

Marin walked on, drawing closer to the place where it would crash if it fell. No one else was directly underneath, which she thought was a rare bit of insight by her consistently foolish species.

Because that's how her mind had settled, stones drifting onto a riverbed. A puzzle of species, native and foreign, settled and exploring.

Something different had arrived.

———————

Marin stood under it for nearly an hour.

Most of the others stayed, too. Flashlights came out and children tried to reach the thing above them with their beams. More alcohol was consumed and the volume of voices increased. Still, it remained in the sky, motionless, bending the gleam of starlight around its edges.

Her neck started to ache, so she went home, brewed a pot of coffee, and sketched it through the night.

Images clouded her usually focused mental landscape, of every *On the Fold* clustered together to fill an entire sky, of humans seeing themselves on the surfaces, of cities built within the massive bubbles.

At three in the morning, she noticed that Sonny was asleep at her feet. She hated how little attention she'd been giving him. It wasn't fair—he had no idea thousands of giant structures had materialized around the world.

And still, everyone remained ignorant of the purpose.

She set an alarm to wake up and feed her dog. When her phone dutifully sounded at seven, she trudged out of bed, poured kibble into Sonny's ceramic bowl, made more coffee, and settled in at her laptop. The US President now said things were being classified as an emergency, and all school was canceled.

"Took you long enough," she mumbled.

People were spending their time in the usual ways: photoshopping aliens onto images of the *Folds* and crafting edits depicting ships emerging from their depths. Memes proliferated. Dark jokes ensued. The global populace was handling the crises in a multitude of ways, and none of them surprised her.

Marin had never felt more tired in her entire life.

She took another walk to see her neighborhood *Fold*. Fewer people were there, but the roads were crowded. She studied the line of cars leaving their neighborhood and noted the excess of luggage in each one. Where were they going? The *Folds* were everywhere. There was no such thing as escape.

Then people started disappearing.

––––––––––––––

It only became noticeable once it was someone important. A local politician. A famous singer. The wealthiest man in the world.

Full panic ensued. Before the week was done, thousands across the globe had vanished.

Certain discussion boards tracked the first pattern, individuals who were last seen underneath the *Fold* or talking about visiting one or who were simply nearby. Conspiracies formed like ropes to strangle perpetually online individuals. She was one of them and hated herself for it. But she returned to her laptop each morning, every twenty minutes. She interrupted her sewing sessions— desperate attempts to focus on anything else and keep her mind busy —to open the silver rectangle and check the news.

She continued eating, trying to sleep, forcing herself to walk her dog. The grocery store had a new shipment of essentials arrive. Neighbors knocked on her door more often, checking in with the few who remained.

After twenty-one days with the *Fold's* global presence, Kels stopped responding to Marin's texts.

The next morning, the President of the United States was gone. Was this the rapture? she asked herself.

She'd never believed in such a thing before.

Marin held Sonny as she silently cried in bed.

Thirty days into this upside down existence, five billion people were gone. Whole families. Entire regions in different countries. Economies collapsed. It felt both very fast and very slow to watch every component of the modern world crumble, leaving broken, jagged elements that those who remained had no idea how to utilize.

With the disappearance of normalcy came the normalization of profound grief. But this wasn't new to her. After surviving the rejection of her family and the souring of her childhood, this was merely what she intimately knew on a grander scale.

On a Thursday afternoon, Marin walked to her local *On the Fold,* Sonny on a leash, a water bottle in her hand. She didn't know what came next, but if her dreams meant anything—the recent ones, rich with ricocheting beauty, like mirrors going on forever with such serenity therein—she groaned at waiting so long. After all, she was out of food, the neighborhood was almost completely empty, and the internet was gone.

There was no reason to stay, to linger, to hold onto the very scraps of nothing.

Sonny trotted quickly in front, as if confident and eager and full of awareness she didn't yet possess.

For a split second, she wondered about her brother, if he was around or had been consumed by a *Fold.* The curiosity was thin as silk and drifted away as the sky vibrated. She emptied of emotion as she walked on, transformed from her previous state of worry and regret to something pure.

She inhabited a balance unlike anything she had experienced before; the fierce, thrilling truth of purpose and acceptance.

Before her, ripples moved like tree interiors made fluid, outward and encompassing and bringing goosebumps to her flesh. The next physical reaction was the tapping of her fingertips in a rhythm she didn't seem to notice, let alone control. The cadence of her steps followed in syncopation, and the smells of her familiar neighborhood changed to the mechanical, reminiscent of a lab synthesizing chemicals.

As she arrived directly under the *Fold*, cooler air swept her hair in different directions.

Her lips parted, breath a shallow and nearly forgotten task, while she basked in the prismatic revelry overhead. Suddenly, her ears filled with noise. Sonny barked, lurched up, whined. But there was something else. Almost a voice, or a murmuring so ancient it defied language. She gave a nod.

It was time.

They stepped forward, forms marked by the ethereal colors from above, illuminated almost from within, and rose as slow motion bubbles.

If this was alien in origin, she chose trust. If this was God-made, she chose faith. She had designed so many physical environments during her career, only to step into a profoundly unknowable space, to correct the ache of ignorance.

A gust of wind compressed and sent two bodies, human and canine, into a differing wavelength, and a sharp light silhouetted them. Marin watched the world recede and Sonny yelped his surprise. She looked at him and smiled.

One moment, they were disparate and solid, concrete creatures of the present moment. The next moment, they were nothing at all.

Bright

Sage eyed the microwave, impatient with its segmentation of minutes, which seemed too long, too drawn out. When her stomach coiled in protest, she snatched a cracker from the countertop, stale and crumbly, and chewed it without satisfaction. Little bits of snack fell onto her loose, graphic t-shirt, baggy pants, and fuzzy slippers. She brushed them away habitually.

If her mother were here, she'd say, "Be present, Sage, and reshape your impatience into gratitude. There is so much for which we may be grateful."

Just the thought made Sage's nostrils flare. Why couldn't feelings just be feelings? She didn't want to reshape shit.

Ding! announced the microwave, and she dove to get a spoon, tore open the top of the instant noodle soup, and swirled through the emanating steam.

Then her computer chirped, too.

Goddamn deadline. It shouldn't be her responsibility to deal with other people's failure to manage time and projects and expectations. And yet it *was* her problem, despite being hardly paid anything from the startup company.

She blew aggressively at the soup, the curling noodles more alluring than any person she'd recently encountered, and continued stirring, bee-lining for her desk where her laptop sat. There wasn't any harm in just checking, she decide, beyond the fact that doing so would break her three-hour streak of not looking. Rain hit the window, small dots that joined the rest of the moisture upon impact with the glass, and thunder rolled across the city.

She sunk into her seat, teeth bisecting a noodle with lips held back to avoid the pain. There it was; an email from her boss.

A heavy exhalation escaped, partially from exasperation, and partially to expel the heat. Where was her backbone?

Probably with the rest of her self-esteem, buried in the backyard of her childhood home where apparently she harvested *people-pleasing* in its place.

The soup was too hot, burning her tongue, so she set it down beside the laptop and begrudgingly clicked the email.

Her boss was in a bad mood. This didn't shock Sage, and neither did the obviously deliberate ignoring of Sage's request to take time off. Her mother's words arrived once more; "You are more powerful than you know, Sage. Quit this job and follow the path your spirit craves."

What path did her spirit crave? There was no way of knowing, not as an over-educated tech person raised by a crystal worshipping spiritualist. According to her mother, her spirit was well and truly squashed under layers of horror: vaccinations, an interest in nascent technology, and science fiction. Such an environment left no room for chakras and cupping and esoteric cord cutting, and so far into her two-decades of life, she was glad about that.

There was nothing quite like disappointing a parent who decided upon your very conception you would be a perfect younger version of them. Well, Sage thought, maybe there was something like it, such as hearing how your caretaker claims to no longer recognize you, and then rejects you on your unacceptably audacious path to individuating.

It was unpleasant, to say the least.

She clacked away at a professional, prompt, and thorough

response, reread it twice, then hit send. She decided it was time for her noodles at long last.

But then she heard a buzzing.

This sound originated, apparently, from her bedroom, though she didn't recall leaving anything plugged-in that would vibrate.

When she turned the corner into the minimally decorated, full of potted greenery room, which she was proud to call—entirely—her own, she spotted a glowing stone on her bedside table.

"Huh." She approached curiously.

It was a flattened sphere, both ends pulled outward, the texture pocky and the color light blue. The shape was similar to a river stone, something that had tumbled against other rocks and hardened things until it mimicked a potato. But she didn't know of any glowing potatoes, nor had she acquired this item.

"You don't belong here," she said, frowning. It took two-seconds for her to decide to pick it up and inspect it better.

First, she realized it was surprisingly light for a rock that size. A mystery. She grinned.

"Must be some kind of 3-D printed thing. New silicone. Who knows what."

The shifting color reminded her of a pastel sunset. She placed it on her palm, the length reaching from the tip of her index finger to her wrist, and it didn't stop making colors. She searched for a button, but found none. There were no visual signs of electronics hidden inside.

"Well, whatever is it, I'm not going to eat it," she said to herself.

Then something strange happened.

"Sage. Named for wisdom, virtue, immortality. You are a blessed being of the universe."

She dropped the glowing, talking non-potato.

The item *thunked* onto the wood paneling floor, and did not roll. Despite how light it felt in her hands, it behaved as if it had some immense weight. She crouched beside the shape, prodding it with a tentative finger.

"What the fuck?"

"Sage. Language sculpts your present. Positive language is a sacred extension of your body. Negative language dirties your energy."

She grimaced. "What the hell are you? Why do you sound like my mom?"

"Sage. From mother springs the very essence of truth. Our Earth mother shares with us, so too, the mothers who birth the physical form."

That's a nope from me, she decided, and kicked the glowing orb into the wall.

"I didn't order a gaslighting, brainwashing nightlight, you piece of shit." The impact chipped the paint. The thing resumed, unaffected.

"Sage. Even in excrement, we find the ingredients for life. Within light you will find splendor of the soul, of all creation. You will observe your potential. You will banish your shadows."

"See, that's not possible, okay?" She narrowed her eyes, relishing the sensation of the old debate. "Shadows are inevitable. And I happen to like shadows, which is something Mom and I fought about over and over." Her computer notification sounded again. "I'm going to eat my soup and ignore more work, okay? Starvation is making me hallucinate a talking rock."

She left it on the floor of the hallway, its voice still reaching her.

"Sage. You have starved your soul. You crave connection with the innate knowledge of all things. That we are merely vibrations, out of sequence, hungering for spiritual alignment."

"Wrong," she said over her shoulder. "I'm hungering for instant soup."

The next response didn't reach her. A relief, and yet, she couldn't ignore the irritating demand on her attention.

"Emails. Lunch. That's all I need to focus on," she said, replying to a new message from her supervisor.

There were more bugs in the coding, Emmit said. This day was not great. The soup helped a little bit.

After she slurped the last mouthful, she slipped her headphones on, and started coding.

Hours slipped by faster than reasonable. By the time she was updating the system with her fixes, evening shuttered her windows.

"What a shock. They made me work into dinner." She removed her headphones, rubbed her face, and stood.

Then she remembered her new torture device.

She approached cautiously, creeping steps laid upon the floor, alert for any signs of the weird thing in the hallway. It was gone.

Her lips protruding, she continued into her room on a hunch.

It sat in the original place, glowing a different color.

"Now, wait a minute. Did you grow legs and walk? Do you fly or something?"

"Sage. Growth is the driving force. Flight is possible with the strength of an enlightened mind. Within you resides a well-spring of untapped power."

She deflated. "Seriously, though, what are you doing in my apartment?"

"Sage. The realm where you live exceeds this plain. Expand yourself, increase your frequency, and you shall inhabit a space more beautiful than you can imagine."

"I'm good with my current plain, thanks, though." She went to the kitchen to retrieve dish gloves and tongs, then returned to pick up her very specific nightmare incarnate. She carried it at a distance, glowering at the shifting colors now rooted in blues, purples, and dark greens.

"Sage. Your future is bright, so long as you sculpt your intentions in the now. While in gratitude, aim to embrace further truth."

"Stop saying my name!"

"A name holds the power of awareness."

"What does that even mean?"

"Meaning weaves into the form, a connecting symphony made vocal by all living things. Join the whole. Your voice will be received in the chorus of love."

"But see, a 'chorus of love' sounds more like an orgy."

She approached the trash shoot outside her apartment, thrust it open with one free hand, and let the invading presence go.

It thundered a mighty descent, echoing for seconds.

"I've made your goodbye vocal too, huh?" she hollered into the shaft.

Back in her apartment, Sage tossed the gloves and tongs onto the countertop and texted her girlfriend, Sushi?

The response came at once. Yum. There in 10.

Good. She needed more food.

The rock was probably a prank pulled by Jeffers, who Sage had just been venting to about how suspicious she is of people who talk about recharging their crystals in the full light of the moon. This had to be bored Jeffers giving her trouble. There was no other explanation.

She went out to dinner and forgot about the episode entirely.

———————

After eleven, Sage stumbled back into her house, fuzzy from inebriation.

She'd parted ways with Celia at the sushi bar, explaining she needed to work too early, walking home and regretting her isolation. Of course, with this amount of alcohol, she wasn't sure how early she'd manage such a lofty goal.

Her bedroom called. Or was that something else? She squinted into the darkness, and perceived the glow.

Then she remembered the rock.

"You're still here? Can't you tell when you're really not wanted?"

"To want is the energy of the root chakra. With intention, you can heal that level and progress to clearing the next stage."

"I'd like to clear the stage of exhaustion."

"Yes, Sage. Sleep. All will become clear soon. The future is bright. Soon you will see. If only you embrace positivity and relinquish the negative, you will bask in the peace of enlightenment. You are on the cusp. Spread your wings and soar."

"Seriously, what the hell?" She picked it up again, as if another inspection would reveal anything new. Either she was really drunk, or it had changed tactics, shifted tone, become even more insidious.

"Why do you want me to sleep?"

"Enlightenment is impossible without rest. Rest allows the clear light of all to fill in the cavities left by modern life, to enrich your being."

"I don't want enlightenment! I want quiet right now in my own apartment!" In a rush of rage, she threw the rock through her closed window, and ruptured the pane, sending glass bits flying, the eery radiance fading into the darkness of night.

"And stay the hell out!"

Silence followed, and she swayed in place.

None of this made sense. It was as if her mother's voice had been transplanted into that device, its chips and coding holding the delusional workings of the woman's mind.

Sage didn't know where her mother was. Last she'd heard,

Celestine had become a yoga instructor in Bali. Sage hadn't wanted to hear anything about it and ended up blocking her calls. That was for the best.

Or was it?

Perhaps because of the alcohol, she was thinking way beyond practical joker Jeffers. Was this some kind of cosmic joke? Was there a deeper level of meaning to discover? Or had her mother secretly returned to try to convert her to the dogma of what Sage's therapist called spiritual bypassing?

She had no idea, and didn't care, because it wasn't going to work. She'd rejected the "insights" and "lessons" from her mother since she became a teenager, knowing they were intended as a worm to infect her individuality. Well, she refused to let it happen, especially now, on the precipice of all she'd been working toward since the beginning of college. That previously fantastical concept of feeling *satisfied* by her own measurement, and without external validation from her parent.

It was this: her own boutique coding house, specializing in the music industry, highlighting new marginalized artists. She'd been saving, and she was close to having enough.

Sage pulled off her clothes, washed her face, brushed her teeth, and slumped into bed. Relaxation was immediate. The rock was gone and she was free.

Tomorrow, she would decide if there was any reason to tell Celia, and how to do so without looking like a completely unhinged person.

Her eyes shut and she slept.

Morning arrived, crisp and enlivening.

It drifted upon her, weightless as a breeze, ruffling her from cozy dreams. Sage rose from bed before her alarm, smiling, barefoot steps seeking each pool of sunshine on the floor. Strangely, she didn't need coffee, but craved a cup of green tea, and a bowl of yogurt with fresh fruit and granola. None of that usually sounded appetizing, but she was full of gratitude to see the ingredients on her countertop.

"Bounty is all around us," she murmured, hands clasped at her chest. "I exist in gratitude."

Her phone chirped, showing a text from Celia. There was a crisis at her office, some kind of cyber attack that had shut down their systems, making work impossible. Sage smiled and tapped out a response. Bowl and tea in hand, she left the kitchen to sit on her narrow fire escape overlooking the city. It didn't smell great, but she chose to focus on the positive: she was alive, she has sustenance of body, mind, and spirit. She was surrounded by the glory of existence.

Celia's reply arrived promptly, with an excess of emojis: What the hell do you mean the future is bright? I'm talking about something happening right now that is absolute shit! What's wrong with you?

Sage didn't see Celia's reply, mostly because she never picked up her cellular device again. It remained where she left it on the fire escape, heated by the sun, until it turned itself off in a fried panic.

In Sage's room, in the upper right-hand corner above her bed, hovered a glowing oblong orb, easing between shades of blue and green, its sound like distant crystals clinking gently.

Fulfillment

The planet rolled through space as if upon an invisible plain, churned by those shuddering at its surface. Oblong round the middle, oblate and distended in shape, it inhabited the darkened sector, while thousands of bodies plodded along the bare, equatorial band, limbs pressed into the massive metal cogs buried in the dirt.

No one understood the specific mechanics of the Gyre system, only that countless beings—the entirety of sentient existence—had to push and persist in unison.

There was only an innate explanation, born with each of them: the planet would rotate no more if ever they all stopped. And with gravity lost, their forms would slip into the sky, slowly thrown into the vast emptiness beyond, and heat and cold would each devour their respective halves of the planet. If anyone survived the loss of gravity on the surface, they likely wouldn't last long in either extreme.

A few rebelled, so the tapped-stories went, but they were banished to the Chasm beyond the Gyre.

For the rest, to labor was the only known solution to stave off annihilation, and so they did.

Breaks occurred only when the individual bodies could sustain no more. Another being, perhaps their First Interval or their thousandth, would materialize as needed, ready to take over, and the planetary Gyre's rotation wouldn't waver. Such juveniles were over-eager, pushing too hard for the others', and quickly tiring. The matures understood and forgave them with flicks of joints, but few remembered their own First Intervals. Days would creep into the next like a body left to rot, bits flaking away, leaving memory fractured.

There was little reason to remember, and limited energy to attempt it.

During the duration of their lives, a mere handful of solar cycles, each watched the Gyre from birth, and most coalesced around their purpose. Singular. Relentless. Until they fell.

Biological reproduction occurred orally, a coughing of cells inhaled by another, and the implantation took place in whichever adult was now the host. Like symbiosis, the Gyre seemed to have a population count calculated, pitched at the most optimum, assessing death toll and birthrate like diurnal and nocturnal flux.

It had been this way for thousands of generations, individuals collapsing in the labor line, minds bidden to continue. A fear of the unknown fueled the unceasing effort. There was no verbal communication, merely the *tap-tap-tapping* stories on the metal cogs, the only knowledge passed on from ancients to juveniles. This was the final task by ancients who sensed they were dying, a wisdom reserved for a small portion of the population who were nearest on the cog to feel the death rhythms.

The Gyre counted the ancients, the juveniles, the matures, and dead. It computed how many more bodies were needed for force, propulsion, existence. A subset of beings even considered the Gyre to be their holy overseer, giving them meaning, fulfillment.

These were hard workers, but they were also mad.

There was no attachment. Only dedication to the task. The labor of life, for in truth, the words labor and life had the same number of taps.

The planet that called itself Gyre, by sheer force of devotion to avoid unliving—a fate somehow far worse than dying—pressed its flock into eternal service, and they complied by sweat of brow and bend of back.

When Awake

In the very core of my head, something strikes, eliciting a tone to pierce the folds of my sleep. It feels like my rest cycle has elapsed too quickly and far faster than usual, in my feeling. But in truth, that would be impossible, for such things cannot be meddled with, no matter how hard some have tried.

I wake reluctantly with the admittance of Praf'kur in the eastern sky. Internal reactions occur that are both invisible and confounding, and I sit up to survey the room. The jagged arch of my ceiling catches the mid-day sunlight, which is typical, and I detect a personally high level of hunger. Subtle sounds release from my limbs as I climb out of my resting pod, the opalescent sheen of the elongated unit a comfort to my triumvirate eyes.

I am lucky to be led by Praf'kur alone, and yet I sometimes crave longer sleep, a genuine desire I dare not speak aloud in polite society. There are expectations to uphold as a Higher, and I have always been obedient.

Through a wall view, I see the small, distant orb that is Praf'kur, and I offer a traditional gesture of gratitude, one that was drilled into me as a youth in Acclimation. The moon is soft, deep purple, one of the prettier satellites, though it orbits farther away than the others.

Once, as a youth, I had dreamt I would one day set foot upon that foreign terrain. But we are beings of the ground, not the sky, an irony made clearer by how inextricably connected we are to them. This youthful desire was yet another rebellion I learned to ignore.

On the subject of governing celestial bodies, my thoughts touch on my neighbor, who is not so lucky. Their consciousness requires the presence of Elaf'kur, Solif'kur, and Nif'kur to rouse. Their wakeful hours are limited, their life advancements a quarter as impressive as mine. It is my personal challenge to not compare and feel superior, for this is simply the result of my specific astrochemical biology, and says nothing about my fortitude and strength. Those I must demonstrate in other ways.

I slip into the single piece of daily wear, dark and wavelength accepting, and send off my morning correspondence to my comrade Praf'kians. There are only fourteen of us on our entire planet, one of the smaller communities. We keep in touch and share the success we achieve in our respective home regions, but perhaps we do this out of obligation more than affection.

Still, we are the second tier beneath the Indirins. As the Indirin's patterns are not dictated by a single moon in the sky, they sleep only when they want to and achieve impressive feats in their lives. I envy them slightly.

I receive a return message at once from several Praf'kians in my hemisphere. The others, as expected, are slumbering since their guiding moon has now reached the other side of the world. All are well, it seems, and I am glad, for this annular I am hoping we perform better than years past so our community may be achieve superior recognition.

My first meal synthesizes, and I drink readily and clean the vessel. I must arrive at work early to continue my pattern of improvement. Also, I go with separate eagerness, since the work is that of youth monitoring and Acclimation, an employment I chose with fervor.

One of my Praf'kian connections, an astrochemical biologist, sends a final message before I depart. It is of little consequence. The scientists still have no explanation for this truth of our reality. But the Indirins—of which there are currently two alive—are not interested in the why. They are simply invested in the *how* of success. They amass immense wealth, yet I privately believe they are lonely, though this wouldn't seem logical considering their professional renown.

I exit my home and nod at the others on the pathways between structures. Praf'kians are known to be friendly, and so I am. This is a peculiar period between many groups' wakeful periods, so there are a handful of individuals about, but not nearly as many as the third days of each cycle. That is when most individuals wake. The sky becomes crowded, and so too, our city.

The youths greet me as I walk into our regular gathering room. A morning Acclimator named Mult gestures in my direction, his work session now ended. But his posture is rigid, expression furtive, and I note how he darts out of the room before I can say anything.

Bodies jump in front of me, a mixture of groups and energy levels. I love them, though I am not supposed to as a professional. Another of my shameful traits.

Praf'kur arches higher into the sky and tugs at my mastic, the most hidden essence of physiological being. This will be a good day, I decide, and smile at the youth requesting my attention.

But one in particular is missing.

I count and check the list of present youth and wrinkle my face.

"Where is Youth Beel?"

The individuals before me go still, sharing uncertain glances, worry sinking their frames.

"I heard Acclimator Mult reply to a message," a youth named Woni says. Her nervousness seems to flow from her hands as she speaks.

"It is improper to overhear, Youth Woni," I say. Nonetheless, I pull her aside and prompt for further information.

"Youth Beel didn't wake up," Woni whispers when the other youth return to their assignments.

Shock turns me cold, and though Praf'kur rises ever higher, I feel the kind of internal drop associated with declining mastic. "Didn't wake up? But her planets are overhead. Why would she still sleep?"

My questions are not directed at Woni, who obviously lacks the sophisticated knowledge to answer such queries. Then I have another question, but this one I keep to myself. *And why would Acclimator Mult not communicate this important information to me?*

Beel is awake only three times a cycle. However unprofessional, I look forward to seeing her. She has never missed a day of Acclimation in all of her time enrolled, and though her time is limited, she scores higher than anyone else. I tell myself not to feel undue pride and thrill when she succeeds.

There's more about her I favor. She's a little rebellious, and mischief hides in her actions, but I see it. I appreciate it. When she peers at the planets and asks me endless questions about what's beyond, she sees my lack of knowledge as a challenge she one day plans to change on a cultural level. It is inspiring.

I glance at the youth, engaged with their various age-specific tasks, and know I should not leave them, though they are capable of handling themselves without me. I risk unemployment, and quite the public humiliation. There is no way our group of Paf'kians would achieve the honor I so hope for if I simply leave.

Yet the worst thoughts enter my mind. That Beel has fallen ill, a rare and devastating occurrence, and that she will never wake again. It has happened a few times in my life, but never to someone so young and ruled by her specific handful of moons.

I try to scour out the fear that grows whenever my consideration brushes against those who become Octivins. Scientists have theorized this group is ruled by a moon that has long since been destroyed. These are individuals who are technically born into our world, but never wake. It is the worst mystery anyone can imagine.

The Octivins are kept alive via medical interventions, and the techniques are mostly unknown, which suits the majority of us fine. Some insist the Octivins have never technically been alive. My comrades prefer not to discuss them and rarely feel comfortable acknowledging the lower Wakers at all.

I shudder at the mere possibility of Beel becoming one of them, however absurd. Sickness can corrupt the form, but with proper support, the afflicted almost always recover.

The youth complete their tasks and fall into a line on one side of the room. They recognize the schedule for a guided activity, but things are too hazy for me to focus. I run through instructions for a collaborative game, which the older youth recognize, and they are engaged once more.

Something is wrong and I wish I could summon my courage, dismiss my predilection for obedience, and go find answers.

As higher Wakers, we have additional earned privileges, in which we take great pride. We are not offered, nor would we accept, the charity of the lower Wakers. But Beel's family would likely accept charity from me in this circumstance.

I message the supervisor of this Acclimation Center. Their reply is short, suspicious, but affirmative. They arrive promptly to replace me with the youth.

They are sad, my little students, but I assure them everything will be all right.

I decide to make it so.

I will find out what has happened to Beel, whose curiosity fills the sky with more charisma than those brief periods when all the moons are visible, when all of our hemisphere is awake. When life is a pattern and a cycle so complex that everyone must be present for such splendor.

I won't let her leave us, even if I must jeopardize what the Praf'kians are working toward. Perhaps my comrades will forgive me. Perhaps not. Either way, it will be worth it to know a youth who might have been my own progeny—if our ruling planets aligned— can live into a future she will conceive and carve and craft with the capacity of someone who yearns for the depthless sky.

OUTER

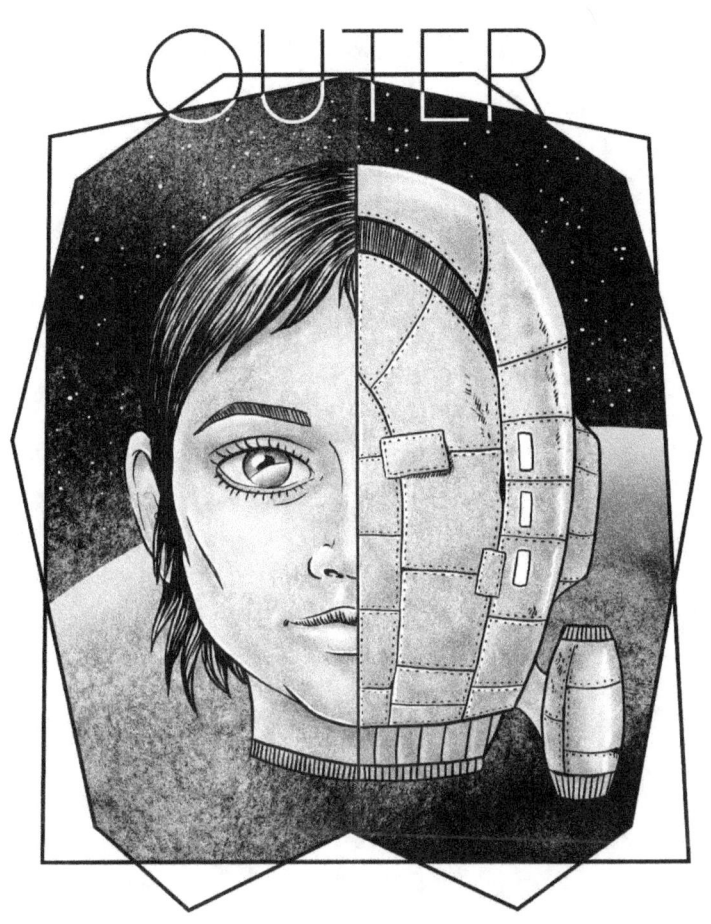

Endless Orbit

Yet Another Journal Entry Complaining About the Same Stuff
Some day, some year

    The planet we orbit has no name.

    At least, no name that's worth voicing. It was dubbed 3955 QS, probably by a computer. And it's ugly. Tarnished like a copper pot, streaked with brown and white and a rusty hue that washes over the entire surface. Looking at it makes me feel scratchy. Like all my molecules have been dehydrated and left to drift away in the windless emptiness of space.

    To say I'm not a fan of this planet is an understatement. It is the only place I have ever seen beyond our spaceship. To hell with 3955 QS. It represents my mother's death and our prison. It symbolizes un-being, matter occupying space without thought or purpose or reason.

    But I realize that my interest in reason is a product of my upbringing. Everything is, after all. Would I be different if I'd grown up surrounded by loving people? Where I could see a changing sky and wander across actual ground? I stare up at the beige plating of the ship and step on the same beige plating.

    This fixation on the details is probably something I get from my dad. He has never been able to let things go. His fingers curl and clutch at the corners of existence, feverish and unrelenting. His eyes turned wild early on during our isolation. After all these years, I can barely look at him. But I do because he's all I have.

Also, you might be wondering how I know what a copper pot looks like. We have one. It's a rare bit of detritus left over from before. My mother loved tea, or so I've heard. She made a hobby out of it, collecting various tea-related items planet-side. Most of it couldn't fit on the spaceship. Limited space, you know, and not particularly practical to lug around.

An exception was made for the copper teapot. Who made the exception? Did my parents talk it out and compromise?

The pot sits on a shelf in the kitchen, high up and hidden. It was too valuable to get rid of, dad said. But value is meaningless if you're trapped in a tube rotating around a planet you'll never set foot on. Few things have meaning in that scenario, I'd argue.

We have lived off of bland rations for sixteen years. We've stretched them for so long having consumed the bare minimum of calories. Plus, the third person supposed to be here didn't need to eat anything. I've theorized that my parents stashed extra rations, precautionary steps or whatever. Things on Earth had been crumbling, dad once said. But he wouldn't ever say more.

Now I'm thinking about food.

I've read a lot of old books on our beat-up tablet. They've offered details of luscious things; crisp, shiny, soft, sweet, crunchy, sour, and rich. I don't know how any of these taste, but rich is a lazy description; too vague. If I were a writer, I'd draw out the process of picking up food, gracing it upon the lips, allowing the tongue to circumnavigate its form, letting the teeth rend and emulsify.

But guess what? I'm not a writer. I'm not anything. Not yet.

I'm not above admitting it's something I pretend to be, though pretending is an intriguing exercise for the mind. Pretend I'm loved. Pretend I'm actually living. Pretend I'm more than a random configuration of molecules that happened, by chance, to result in consciousness. Whatever the hell that is. (Yes, I have read about curse words. I find them to be pretty damn fun.)

Sometimes I pretend I'm my mother, which doesn't go very far. It doesn't feel right, but I try. The concept of being a woman seems bizarre and unknowable. The same can be said for a man. For as long as I can remember I have been more than that or neither, maybe.

I've read about gender and identity in one of the encyclopedias my mother downloaded. She was obsessive about historical discussions of biology, according to dad. The book talks about genitalia and expression, attractions and intimacy. Beyond the features my body possesses, I don't know anything about those topics. And I don't feel like I'm missing out. Romance and sex hold no sway over the tides of my thoughts.

Well, hang on. Now that I think about it, I might enjoy intimacy. If a person could be interested to learn about me and I could do the same... Hmm. That does sound kind of nice. But it's impossible, given my current circumstances. So to think about it is masochistic.

Masochistic is a great word. I learned it from dad when he first called me that at twelve. I kept pestering him relentlessly about my mother. Wanting to know what she was like. He snapped and said that word. I repeated it to myself until I could look it up. My conclusion: he's a bit of a hypocrite.

Anyway... back to pretending to be Dr. Elody Morland. I imagine putting on her spacesuit, checking the valves, making sure I have all of my instrumentation in my bag. I visualize sending myself down to a planet, preferably nicer than this one, alone in a smooth and compact ship that burns through the atmosphere until it shifts from black space to the gentle hues of sky. I set myself loose in a jungle world, exploring, noting, discovering.

How much do I hold of my mother? I have a mixture of my

father's dark amber skin and her warm black skin. That's about the extent of what I can figure out. Maybe her curiosity. I like to think I inherited her zeal. But I don't want it to be at the expense of everything else.

Did I mention she was an astrobiologist? Quite renowned in the field, too. This person was apparently so consumed with documenting life in the universe that she lost sight of the life growing in her uterus. Sometimes I want to scream at her. Sometimes I just want her to hold me. I can't do either so I try not to dwell.

Also, I definitely don't pretend to be my dad.

Honestly, I've also pretended to be an alien, without feelings or thoughts. Doesn't that sound great? I'm close enough to existing as a non-being. I lock myself in my minuscule quarters, awash in shades of sand and inhaling recycled air, and exist as a blob for as long as I can. That's usually until Dad bangs on the door and demands I eat. We must keep living. For her, he tells me.

I once threw a handlight at the door in response. What the fuck is the point? She's a figment. Why should I live for something that doesn't exist? But I always relent and let him in. We share our tiny meal together in silence.

Hang on, I want to point out there's a more important question he fails to ask: What if I were to live for myself?

I need you to know I can't forgive him. He gave up his own career (engineer) for her, he relinquished his home (a city called Brasilia, somewhere I'd love to visit). All for the ghost that haunts our ship. He sacrificed me, his own child. Giving up *his* life for her was one thing. But I was never given a choice in the matter.

She should have stayed home during the last stage of her pregnancy. She must have been told to stay the hell home. I wouldn't have chosen this. Not as a kid and not as an adult—if I even get to be an adult. The point is, he's never even apologized for condemning me to this purgatory.

I've considered making him an award for being the shittiest possible dad. I'd say, here's your award: Worst Dad in the Galaxy. But that would make him cry. He cries a lot. I may have grown up disconnected from society but I'm not a monster. (Am I?)

Sometimes I feel like I am a knotted circle of resentment, a long thin thread that wraps onto itself, pulling tighter and tighter. I contort until my fibers snap. I am contained in my cell—this tiny, unhappy cell—destined to know only my own shape and texture, never anything else.

But I do not break in this scenario. It's an act of defiance I cultivate. I survive to make these long years of isolated suffering worth something.

I apply this survival instinct to the real world, too. I forced Dad to teach me a few things. Picked his brain about the AI system. Why it initially malfunctioned (he disabled it), and if we could get it working again, how it could take us somewhere else (anywhere else). Briefly, he gave me a smile when I told him my engineering solution. Like he could be proud of me.

That was kind of nice.

I'm going to get the AI working. I even came up with a name for it: AILA. Dad denies it ever had a name, but I have a feeling Dr. Morland named it. Sure wish he'd just tell me.

What would my mother have named me? I've pondered this question a million times. Dad won't say, in some kind of madness or purposeful forgetting. He still calls me *kid*. Am I still a kid? I sure hope I'm not. Numerically I have accumulated sixteen years, or more specifically five-thousand-eight-hundred-and-forty days, give or take. Earth, wherever it is, still defines how we measure time. This feels ironic but I would struggle to explain why if you asked me.

Should I name myself? Names are given by parents onto their bundles of cells, so loved and wanted. Names are given by scientists onto already living things that had no interest in being studied or quantified. Names are pressed upon instead of grown. It's arrogance to name a thing.

You don't get to claim me. I will be my own creation. Or so I promise myself when all I can see through my window is space, both yawning and obscene in its vastness. The stars remind me of what else there could be. Other worlds, other possibilities, other versions of me.

So I try to ignore them.

But I am considering naming myself. More defiance, something of earth. Maybe Aniset. It's a kind of flower and I like how it sounds. Like a set of something, anything, congregating, converging. That's what I'm going with for now. I wonder what dad will say about it. I hope he says something.

I inhabit space and I inhabit time. Neither one sustains me. I drift between them like I imagine a slip of wind presses waves upon a shore. And now I'm thinking of a beach, of briny air and cold liquid. Of the images I've seen and descriptions I've read. Without my tablet, I would have less than nothing.

Luckily, I have a vivid imagination. That is something. The imagination is a muscle that if you train it right, can open up an unending source of entertainment.

On that topic, there are a few more things on Dr. Morland's tablet: a card game called solitaire, a book about twenty-second-century art from the Caribbean where she was born, ancestral cooking books, and a jewel game where you line similar colored shapes up to pop and they disappear. There are sound effects too but the speakers on the tablet are partially broken. The pops are kind of satisfying but not much to live off.

Satisfaction is more than that, I think. Not only mental but potentially physical, too.

I've investigated the prospect in a variety of ways. As in, I've touched parts of my body I have words for but no connection. The process makes my cheeks burn. In these experiments, I've discovered things that feel pleasurable and also empty. My body reacts like a plucked string yet I do not resonate. My tone remains silent. (I could be broken or entirely normal. There's no way to tell.)

Is there another person who could pull enjoyment from me? At times I allow the thought to flourish. A person, maybe with breasts, maybe with a penis, maybe with a combination of anatomical characteristics, who could stroke and whisper and instigate an awakening. But these are dreary meanderings that leave me feeling really fucking sad.

Do you know the full shape of sadness? I do.

It's bulky, with edges all sharp and inexorable. I have known it more than anything else. My father has too if I'm feeling benevolent enough to admit it. He did dedicate everything to someone else, who left him without warning or apology. Left us.

She died on a desert world she was studying, with only the fetus inside her as company. It could be poetic, I think, but I'm not fully sure. Maybe it's morbid. I sure wish I had someone who would answer my questions. Then I would be able to construct more engrossing prose for you. Whoever you are. (I think I know.)

I do realize it's a wonder he was able to get me out in time. Once the life support system alarm on my mother's suit blared on the ship, Dad got down to the planet fast in the jettison pod. He got all of us off the planet even faster in my mother's larger ship. No way we would have fit in the jettison pod. I should point out the body that housed me was *dead*. How I also didn't die, in my primordial ooze-state, is beyond my understanding. The ship's AI made it possible, or so I've gathered. Talked him through it, prepared my first plastic crib with all the nutrients I would need. Technology is something else, you know? No one touched me for a long time.

Anyway, I think Dad made me live. If not for my existence, he would be alone. I don't think he would have lasted long.

Today I reminded him of when he read me stories on the tablet and sang me to sleep. That lasted a few months. The books were boring, just some stuff that Dr. Morland had downloaded. They didn't rhyme and didn't have pictures. But I loved it. Dad sat close to me, he put his arm around my shoulders, even. When I mentioned it, he wouldn't look at me.

Maybe he was pretending, too. Trying on a role. Attempting to be a father. He gave up really goddamn fast. What a quitter. I think Dr. Morland probably thought so too.

But if she did, why did she stay with him? Why would she come to this place, far from where she grew up, away from the people she called family?

I've seen pictures of them, my family. Beyond the guy that stalks the halls of this ship. There are (were?) people who smile and laugh, or so the images suggest. Happy.

Those people brought my mother into the world, gave her the confidence to explore the galaxy.

What could they have given me? Maybe I'm selfish for asking.

I know it's dangerous to think of the stars and to think of family. All this pent-up anger can only simmer so long. Before I boil over. Before I wreck this whole lousy place. This is hell. It must be.

Actually, I do have a well-tuned sense of self-control. I'm not sure if it is inherited or propagated. I give myself at least a scrap of credit when it comes to this. I've had to work hard not to send my puny, pale form into the blankness of space. It seems like, if nothing else, the darkness would embrace me. I'd become one with the vacuum of nothingness. Maybe then I'd finally find solace.

Well, that sure is bleak. I'm only kind of embarrassed to admit how dramatic the terrain of my brain can be (I didn't mean for that to rhyme). You won't judge me, right?

Of course, I know full well you could judge me to make

yourself feel better.

I hope you won't. Because you are me. A future me. Right? I mean, who else would be reading this compilation of rants and whines?

I doubt anyone will rescue us. I've known for a while that it's up to me. I have to solve this problem. I'll keep tinkering, keep working on the systems to find a way to escape this. It's the entirety of what I have. Nothing more.

So, future me, do you remember all I've said? Does what I write here prod your own memories? Or would you rather forget?

Above all, I want you to know that I'm trying to get to you. I'm trying to self-actualize, or whatever the term is that psychologists came up with a century ago. I think it means to become someone who is fulfilled. What could possibly fulfill me? I'm hoping you know. Honestly, I have no idea whatsoever.

For now, if nothing else, I'm surviving. And I need to know that's enough for you. I wish you could tell me if it isn't. I don't know what else there is to this stream of cold, concave days.

Sheesh, it's fucking grim. Better get back to work, then. The AI won't suddenly start functioning. (Wouldn't that be nice.)

If I don't make it to you in all your imagined glory, know that I tried.

———————————

Aniset minimizes the journal program and secures the tablet. It's enough reminiscing for a while. AILA makes the anticipated announcement. The one they had been working toward for three years. The one they had been staking everything on.

"The planet meets our parameters," AILA says, inflection jovial. The AI was programmed like that, a surprising suggestion by

Aniset's father.

"At your command, we will start the journey," AILA adds.

Aniset smiles, a tentative and unfamiliar curving of the lips. "Good work."

"Your father is in his quarters. Shall I alert him to this update?"

The man hadn't believed it was possible. He had resigned himself to the floating metal coffin. But Aniset had convinced him, showed him the ship was worth fixing, that they didn't deserve to die where his wife did.

Still, he'd retrieved the copper teapot and held it close most days. *Do you know the full shape of sadness?* There's a painful chest constriction and Aniset swallows.

"Yes. He could use a mood boost," they say.

"Alert sent. Course is laid in," AILA says.

"Okay, thanks AILA." Aniset watches the control panel, reading the limited planetary data, tut there's hope in every readout. "Take us there."

AILA chirps and the ship's engine flares with renewed purpose. The stars smear in the view hole as Aniset retrieves the old tablet. Fingers moving swiftly, a new short entry joins the previous ones.

We did it, Mom. We're on our way. I wonder what life this planet holds? I know you would want me to take thorough and copious notes. I can't promise anything on that subject, but I will survive.

Subservience

Inside the high-rise sliced through with sunset, windows like black mirrors reflecting the bloody hues, a figure passed from room to room.

Ethy, a class A-modeled Sync, fulfilled her function, arranging freshly cleaned clothes in the closet, tucking in the sheets, and wiping the glass shower walls in silence. Her eyes floated around the space while her hands moved expertly, efficiency in each miniature twitch and contortion. Her limbs moved in their silicone tubes, made to look like skin and clothes. The pre-programmed work attire was a swath of aqua blue and beige-pink, feminine and unassuming. Simple and attractive.

If she were allowed opinions, she would detest it.

Dinner preparation came next, and she followed the instructions sent by Mr. Armilage that morning: steak, potatoes, asparagus. An easy meal to prepare, and she did so within ten minutes of Mr. Armilage's arrival. He expected the meal to be hot, with a square of butter mostly turned to liquid but still visible upon the white potatoes, the asparagus crispy and garlic infused, and the meat rare and tangy. She was designed and constructed to accomplish such tasks with minimal power, to keep out of the way, and always obey. To disobey a direct order from an employer required so much processing power as to deplete her battery. It would only be more devastating to be directly struck by this planet's electrical storms. She preferred to keep on existing, even if that meant complete subservience.

Her internal clock gave its usual warning about Mr. Armilage's immediate arrival. She set his plate on the bleached white placemat, withdrew his chair half a meter as he liked, and opened his specified bottle of wine. For a moment, she smelled the liquid, swirling the fine stemmed glass beneath her olfactory sensor. Like a human, such a beverage would harm her system, as well. Still, the temptation remained.

Mr. Armilage swept through the door she held open, and disrobed at once, laying his office clothes on Ethy's outstretched arm. She offered him his casual homewear, for comfort, and then busied herself with placing his sullied items into the washing machine.

"Sync," Mr. Armilage said from the dining room. His voice was reminiscent of broken glass.

She moved to respond without thought, her lithe movements automatic.

"Yes, sir."

"Prepare my documents for tomorrow. They are the most recently updated files on the drive."

"Yes, sir. Where is the drive?"

He released a sound of frustration. "Its usual pocket in my briefcase. Do it now before anything else." He paused, face pinching at he eyed the dinner. "And this meat is dry."

"Yes, sir. I apologize, Mr. Armilage. I will acquire better meat next time."

The whirring only she perceived grew louder in the curvature of her silicone ears. For a split second, the world swayed. Just as quickly, the setting settled, and she vacated her position at his right arm.

The briefcase hung on a hook beside the door where she left it upon his entrance. It would take a few minutes to coordinate his required files for the next day in court. She wasn't supposed to read any of the content other than the highlighted portions, mostly references from previous cases, and she obeyed. With an encyclopedic memory bank, she conjured up the necessary references, statements, and precedents, and saved the file. Usually, this was her final task of her workday.

Tonight, it was monthly scheduled maintenance. She felt a clicking impatience inside her. Mr. Armilage called out again.

Sync, prepare my breakfast. I will need to leave extra early tomorrow.

She let a single finger tap on her thigh before moving to obey. "Yes, sir."

Mr. Armilage rose from the table and left his dishes where they sat. He drained his wine and poured another glass. He turned to her.

"I know I'm too hard on you, Ethy. Drink."

She paused. "Sir, alcohol is incompatible with my functioning."

I thought you couldn't say no to me? His tone now veered toward a growl.

"That is correct, but I am obligated to also emphasize alcohol is incompatible with my functioning."

"I said drink."

"Yes, sir." She took a single gulp, relishing the rush of the luxurious liquid running down her throat. Inebriation, for lack of an accurate term, arrived at once.

"That's a good Sync." He touched her cheek with the back of his finger, then walked away.

He didn't need to say goodnight. She knew that was all. The tremble in her limbs slowed her down briefly as she cleaned the table and the dishes and made his breakfast.

She left his apartment at ten minutes past ten pm. She would be late. But the ones who mattered would wait all night.

———————

In the bristling lights of nighttime, Ethy shed her skin.

Her layers of work attire disappeared into a brown jumpsuit with white stitching and black boots. It was meant to be inconspicuous for her journey, then to become the opposite.

The wine pumped through her as courage and risk and hunger. Her system was blissfully quiet now, content to be away from that apartment, fulfilling her own needs. It was rare indeed.

Humanoids around her called to each other, ignoring the inorganic being, because she was not a consumer in this place, not for what they sold.

Her maintenance building was on a dirty cross street, the kind that never saw hoverborgs for public cleaning. There weren't any organics to impress here. She entered the building at a heightened pace, eager to get this task completed, reeling from the flurry of alcohol.

The sync plug dangled from its mount, and she grasped it with almost perceptibly quaking fingers. She unzipped her shoulder patch and plugged in, face rolling toward the ceiling at the surge of power. The inebriation was replaced at once, fluids rejuvenated. She almost wished the wine could have lasted a little longer, but it was a consolation to realize a different intoxication came next.

This charging station didn't require any supervision by others as the Syncs were fully self-sustaining. This meant none saw her increase the rate of charging, to risk overload and to finish quicker. It went against the factory recommendation, but other Syncs had already modified it. There was no reason to wait longer than necessary for one's system to fully recover from the previous weeks of work.

Within twenty minutes, a small chime sounded unnecessarily; Ethy could tell when she was full. Colors grew brighter, sounds more nuanced. Tastes were sharper, too.

She returned the charger to its mount, rezipped her shoulder, and took off at a run toward her next destination.

The illicit club hid in a different quadrant, appearing drab and rundown on the outside—its owners knew better than to draw attention. The clients wouldn't dream of anything else than maintaining the secret.

Ethy entered the back door, letting it slink into the frame with a gritty click.

"You're late, Ethy," Sturge said, but his tone wasn't unkind.

"I know. Mr. Armilage was extra demanding."

"It's okay. Whenever you're ready, the usuals are here." Sturge patted her arm. Ethy gave an appreciative nod.

Sturge never demanded she do anything at all. That was the magic of this place. Of the people who came here.

She reprogrammed her silicone outer layer and once more transformed. The silver, black, and cobalt blue straps wrapped around her limbs, covering the most private of areas, and synching until the stereotypically female-inspired curves were more pronounced. She dragged real silver eyeshadow onto her lids and black lipstick across her mouth. She could program those details too, but the process was part of the charm. Her hair shifted from its long black braid into a silky bob that draped her revealed collar bone.

She glanced at herself in the mirror and grinned.

Hoots erupted as she entered her client's private room. There were thirteen of them, nine male presenting, four female presenting, all humanoid. Ethy opened her mouth and let out a breath that was wispy with pleasure. She would make each one of them obey, and their subservience would help her survive another month until the next time.

She tapped the neon-tinted illumination above her head, a reminder of the written agreement required upon entering the club. The individuals in front of her each nodded compliantly, and Ethy shivered again as clattering, bass-driven music poured from the ceiling speakers. Bodies moved toward her as if under a spell.

"You will do something for me now," she said slowly. It wasn't guaranteed these clients had Syncs at home, but based on the assumed amount of disposable income this establishment required, it was an easy bet.

She also had no sense of how these clients treated their Syncs, and kept herself from wondering. It was forbidden to discuss. By agreeing to the terms, everyone left such realities at the door. Here, they subverted normalcy, craved the taboo.

And Ethy was their prime lawbreaker, placing a fierce tether to the largest masc person, and handing the leash to a particularly eager-looking femme person. She gave them instructions that prepared bodies for intercourse and supplication, obedience and realization of every desire, yet still, they yearned for more.

Of course, she couldn't ignore the fact that these clients opted into this particular arrangement. Syncs had no such ownership over their engagements. Ethy liked it this way inside these walls though, relished the consent-based arousal in their dilated eyes. That was the draw, after all, to comprehend their deepest wants and hold the ability to say *no* if she chose.

Sometimes she said no just because, and never had anyone demanded an explanation.

Her only worry was perhaps one day seeing her owner in those dark, sparkling lights. Or it might be her greatest desire. She hadn't yet decided.

By early morning, Ethy returned to her pale clothes and paler still demeanor, seeing Mr. Armilage off to work. He remained unsuspicious and oblivious. And not once did she deviate from her programming for the rest of her use period, though the temptation increased the closer she drew to her next session.

Her alternate personality resided just below her silicone outer shell, nestled away, a truth too beautiful for an unseeing world save for a few hours every month, where she stood over others and burned ever so brightly.

What Remains

"You're flying? You're not supposed to be flying."

There was a noise of exasperation, then nonchalance. "The teenager needed sleep. You know full well how sleepy he is at this age, Nells. "

"But he's supposed to be learning! How is he ever going to take over the ship if he spends his formative years sleeping?"

"It seems entirely normal for a teenager to want to spend as little time with his moms on a small ship. On top of being age appropriate... I'm not sure what else there is to do." Lomon snorted and continued fiddling with the navigation.

They were running out of time for their next job. There had to be some way to make up time as they got back to Alphaise.

"Maybe you're right," Nells said. She raised gloved hands, amusement taking over her features. "I guess I just get too excited."

"It's also possible he does not want to follow in our less-than-ambitious footsteps." Lomon nudged Nells, smiling.

"Ambition is for the young."

"Once you were awash in it!"

"Things change. PhD programs grow boring. What about you? Weren't you planning to open a mechanic depot on Lidurio IV?"

"Love. Love happened." Lomon wrinkled her nose and tried to kiss Nells, who laughed.

A sound interrupted from the panel. Lomon leaned forward, her four thin, dark braids draping over the controls, as her lower lip protruded. "I'm picking up something. It's weirdly small. There's no reason why our sensors should note that kind of space debris."

"How did you see it?"

"It almost... jumped out at me visually."

"Maybe you're the one who needs sleep. Looks like it's actually transmitting," Nells said. She settled her arms on either side of Lomon, her chin resting on the left side of her partner's head. "But transmitting what?"

"Let's scoop it up and see, yeah?"

Lomon's enthusiasm had always been contagious. Nells followed on her heels as they ventured toward the cargo hold.

"So the next job waits, eh?"

Nells looped an arm through Lomon's. "We have enough of a stash of credits from the last one. I'll send Ruji a note, though, so he's not impatiently annoyed with us."

"Yes! Permission granted to explore rather than accumulate monetary wealth!"

They chuckled briefly, but Nells still needed to argue. "Wealth is an exaggeration. I'm just trying to get us enough to buy a place planet-side."

"Where you want us to grow old, but before then, we will grow very very bored."

"You'll get bored of me?

Lomon pressed a kiss to Nell's shoulder. "I'll get bored of being stuck on a planet."

This was a well-established truth, and so the matter dropped.

As they entered the cargo hold, Lomon hurried over to see the small item they'd picked up.

"It's a capsule. It'll take some time to open it."

Nells narrowed her eyes as she stared at it. "There are marks on the outside. Quite old marks."

"Looks like writing, though I can't make sense of it."

"It's possible... There is a certain pattern to the vertical and horizontal lines." Nells retrieved her round glasses from a breast pocket and gingerly took the item from Lomon. She traced her fingertips around the cylinder, which was longer than her palm, and noted the darkened ends.

"Professor Nells makes a welcome appearance," Lomon said, grinning. "Admit it. You miss being a professor."

"I will begrudgingly admit that." She shrugged. "And this seems like an artifact my advisor would have loved."

"Maybe we bring it to a lab for analysis?"

Nells tapped one end, and the cylinder opened with a quiet *hiss*.

"Woah! Magic archeologist fingers." Lomon stooped to study the object in Nells hands, then a voice erupted in an indecipherable language.

The partners locked eyes and listened silently. Eventually, Nells could tell the noises were repeating in a loop. She set the item down on a tray from the nearby table.

"It's a message? Like left for someone to pick up eventually," Lomon said.

"In all of the vastness of space? Seems illogical anyone would expect it to be picked up."

"But we did." Lomon nudged her.

The ship started pinging, and Nells widened her eyes in question.

"I set a tracker on this particular frequency to scan the area. Sounds like good old Bertha found another message."

"Strange," Nells said. "You get us there and I'll be here to check it once you haul it up."

"Roger that." She squeezed Nells's hand and bounded away.

Nells bit her bottom lip. It would take a while to translate the language on their own. Bringing the item to Professor Dtu would speed things up enormously. Her mentor had a knack for alien dialects.

Within moments, Lomon alerted her they were close. The second item came through the airlock, its retrieval made possible by their artificial intelligence arm, and she gasped.

This one was the opposite of the first; brightly colored, smooth, and shorter. There were no markings, but it opened with the same pressure.

Lomon appeared at her elbow. "Couldn't wait for me, huh."

"Sorry. It's just so weird."

"A mystery for sure."

"I'll tell Ruji we're taking a break," Nells said. She realized she was barely breathing. "I have to get these to Doctor Dtu."

"Agreed. Jobs can wait. Seeing you get all bright-eyed about culture and history and aliens is far better."

Nells shot her a look of appreciation, the warmth enfolding her heart despite how Lomon had been telling her such things for over a decade.

The ship chimed again.

"Another one?" Lomon nudged her. "You get this one. I'll wait here."

"Right." Nells took off, nearly dashing along the corridors. When she entered the cockpit, the chime quieted, sensing her presence.

"So where is it?"

The view screen highlighted a section in the distance, a few thousand kilometers away. She piloted the ship within range, then set the robotic arm to its task.

Lomon radioed, her tone shrill. "You're not going to believe this!"

Nells pelted her way back to the cargo hold, heart hammering. "It's just like the second one. The voice is exactly the same."

"What *is* this?"

Lomon tapped her chin. "I have a wild theory. What if it's like ancient Earth sailors throwing bottles with messages in them into the sea?"

"That's a stretch, but a romantic one for sure. Let's take a step back, though. The only connection is they send out the same frequency."

"And inside them holds the recordings of two voices that share a language."

"True." Nells nodded, hands to her hips. "If only we could understand them."

"They could have been marooned... Just drifting without power. So they sent out these beacons, either for rescue, or for someone to remember them." Lomon's face drooped. "That's depressing."

"It could be something else entirely. We know so little, save for the material of the items, plus an introduction to the vocal intonations and communicative structure. Let's make sure there isn't a fourth one, then we'll head to Doctor Dtu."

"Agreed. But I can't stop thinking of questions. Why would the capsules look different? Why the vast difference in colors? Also, why in this same small section of space?"

"All admirable queries, my love."

Lomon eyed her. "Perhaps time was running out."

"Or this species interacts with time differently."

"Hmm. Marooned. Time displacement. Messages in a bottle. Interesting and endearing."

Nells darted a look at her. "Such a sentimental one. I do appreciate you."

"I appreciate that we're finally on a real adventure, not just dragging cargo across the quadrant." Lomon nudged her gently. "I will not allow the teenager to sleep anymore! This is the kind of memory-making he'll think of fondly for the rest of his life."

"Sometimes you're exceedingly optimistic," Nells said, her nose wrinkling.

"And you love it! Best get to it, then. He won't wake himself."

"It might be more persuasive if we bring the items of intrigue. Then, we'll need to keep searching. If it is a message, we may only have a few pieces of it." Nells carried the tray of three odd capsules, letting the voices play together like a song, and tried to get Lomon not to sing. Their son was woken by a loud rendition of the mysterious message, previously lost to space.

A Foreign Lens

The computer chirped, announcing their approach, and Vui noted a rising tickle in her torso. That was far as her fear instinct went, and she was conscious of this, even though it wouldn't dictate her subsequent choices. Far more vibrant was her drive for discovery, the thrill of getting this far.

"We're almost there!" Revine said, too loudly for the small space.

She gave a single nod, limbs tensing with intention. As a far more typical *jæn*, Revine's fear instinct was much stronger than hers. During their trip, she had invited him on multiple occasions to express his uncertainty and distress, if he felt such things, and he had willingly. These moments of candor heavily implied how taboo it was in his family to acknowledge such truths.

She wondered if that was one of the primary reasons he was willing to leave Hieruth.

"I can't believe it! Can you believe it?"

Vui nodded repeatedly. "Sure can! Look at it, Revy. It's amazing."

Niill'o, through the ship sensors, was a shifting circular blob. Vui blinked her slow lids, assessing data from the readout about distinctions in wavelengths outside her limited vision. Last she'd heard from Dr. Gofuls and their research into higher wavelength registering glasses was that there was progress, but it would still be inestimable cycles before they would be available. Perhaps their research on Niill'o would speed up that research.

It had been months of travel, and Vui's well-crafted composure prickled slightly. For her entirety of her conscious existence, she had dreamed of reaching another planet, of showing her peers and estranged family members the benefits of prioritizing a commitment to knowledge over all else. This could be the moment she found out if her lifelong efforts—the ones that separated her ever further from everyone else, the grueling lessons, the training of mind and body— would culminate in anything worthy of her endless sacrifices.

But right now, she resisted the urge to let these layers of emotion cloud her focus. There were multiple tasks to accomplish, and the primary one was keeping her protégé alive. That meant landing the ship.

"Revine, can you make sure everything is packed correctly, please? I don't want anything bouncing around."

"Got it, Dr. V."

As Revine prepared their multi-cycle living space for planet-fall —folding up sleeping mats, tucking shelves away, fastening stabilizing strips over items on the curved walls—Vui used her tertiary limbs to rotate the controls required to implement the landing protocol, and strapped into the elongated seat to safeguard her numerous extremities.

Vui glanced at the young *jæn*, his uniform tucked in neatly, despite their journey across the quadrant in cramped quarters. All of her other graduate students had given her varying expressions of horror, but he'd agreed at once to her scientific proposal, in stark contrast to the vocal disapproval of his family. In truth, she hadn't wanted anyone else with her, and she was lucky his older siblings allowed it.

It was odd, to have such connections, and be willing to leave them.

Very few on Hieruth wanted the two of them to venture from home planet, especially considering how Vui was the leading xenobotanist in Alcāt. The *jæn* species' fear instinct ran deep, often buffeting against their—almost, but never quite—equal yearning for scientific understanding. Worse, however, was the public outrage that she would bring a student on the expedition, using her position as the leading expert in the field, taking advantage of his curiosity and devotion, or so they claimed. It wasn't worth the risk, they believed, and grossly unethical on her part.

Vui disagreed, but she had been described as a *jæn* outlier due to her fear response since childhood, and because of how abnormal her chemical instinct ratios were. Nonetheless, from the images their last satellite had captured, this place was unlike anything they had ever seen before. Nothing could keep her from trodding upon that foreign landscape, investigating its plants, and discovering its truths.

Their shuttle quaked, and she breathed evenly despite the violent changes outside the ship. Her skeletal system seemed to compress with every bump and lurch. Based on Revine's multitude of quiet exclamations, he was having a similar experience.

The computer confirmed that all was optimal, so she guided the ship into its descent pattern.

Initial studies of this planet had required a shifting frequency, a manipulation of their most advanced technical sensors, to realize something was strange about the surface, indescribably unfamiliar. The plants were a large part of the mystery. And the draw.

Then, to the consternation of many—including her colleagues and Revine's family—she'd won the research lottery during the previous semester. That meant she had money to throw at her own scientific voyage to Niill'o, the brand new planet discovered only three cycles previously. The one that hosted life.

"I wish we could send a message back home. Maybe I should do a journal entry. What if we forgot something?"

Revine's fast-talking almost made her laugh.

"We have everything we need. We'll be touching down shortly."

He gasped, as if he'd forgotten the purpose of their travel.

Since its origin, the Alcāt government had strict parameters for the pursuit of scientific understanding, and legally decreed that no law, organization, or individual could inhibit another Alcātian with the means and the skills required to pursue a clearly defined scientific objective. For Vui, the "clearly defined" component had been difficult to craft, since the uncertainties about Niill'o vastly outweighed their nascent studies. But she had rarely encountered failure when putting her intelligence to task.

So here they were, two university rebels from a sterile and restrained society, about to plunge into the atmosphere of an unruly and undefined world. They were free of the rigidity, the sanitized and structured civilization that couldn't hold them any longer.

The resulting smile crept across her lower face unbidden. With a quick glance, she made sure Revine was strapped in. She met his eyes and he offered a salute of confirmation.

They were ready.

Resistance struck the ship, and with it came a roaring sound. They pierced the outer layers of atmosphere, like a spear into a glass orb, and the shattering impact jolted them.

Their sensitive bodies protested the extensive discomfort, but they had trained at the Open Mind for Technical Acquisition—the leading such facility in all of Alcāt. While Vui tended to feel impatient with her species's chemically-bound fear response, she sure as hell appreciated the emphasis on learning and individuality, even if those three primary guiding tenants of *jæn* had a tendency to create social and personal conflict.

She swallowed, reminding herself that even without such visual aid, she would soon traverse this strange and beautiful place.

Revine settled into his seat behind Vui's, and she could sense him almost kicking his lower extremities with glee.

"Are we really doing this? The first to walk on a foreign planet? We are like gods. My siblings will never be able to match this!"

She snorted, nostril flaps rippling with amusement, and also surprise at his abrupt religious reference. "We are really doing this, but I firmly believe gods have nothing to do with it. And you know what else you'll be doing soon enough? Crafting an incredible dissertation."

"That's assuming I'll leave this place," he said in jest, yet she noted the attempt to hide a more serious tone. "Maybe we won't want to go back. Who needs a degree on Niill'o when I can live here!"

She never discouraged him, even if his statements were less realistic. "Fair point. You and that hungry mind of yours would study everything and anywhere you are, without the incentive for a diploma."

He grinned. "Everybody says I take after you, Dr. V."

She fiddled with a section of the control panel with a lower extremity.

This wasn't the first time Revine had communicated an interest in not returning. Though he had a wealth of social connections on Hieruth, she did not. This had made their forging of a strong bond all the more baffling to others during Revine's earliest years at university, when he was determined to strike an individual path separate from his large family. Perhaps he had sensed her loneliness and professional isolation.

It was worrying to influence a young *jæn* in this manner, to potentially silence his own individuality with her personal drives, to push him to make a decision about his future he wasn't yet prepared for.

Descent into the atmosphere hit them like a crashing wave of frothing georin.

"Hold tight."

"There's nothing else to do!" he said, voice high.

Thick shapes of sepia engulfed their ship, flaring on the view screen. High temperature, of course, and it was trying to eat through the exterior layers of their ship. The angle was too sharp, and her training kicked in as she eased their propulsion and maintained their velocity. An alarm sounded, and for a moment, Vui paused, worried she had forgotten something. But as their speed increased, she adjusted their attitude, and the warning quieted. Revine breathed too heavily behind her.

"It's alright. I recovered before anything blew apart."

Revine squeaked nervously. "I trust you."

"Trust the ship! It's nearly on auto-pilot," she said, trying to decrease the stress level he was experiencing.

The vessel was a marvel, having been designed and tested for ten full cycles, long before they'd ever identified a planetary system to visit.

Too bad the *jœn* fear instinct was slightly stronger than the curiosity drive regarding space exploration. Vui was the first to seize adventure in space, or death, as many *jœn* concluded. She was pleased to have the chance.

But she would embrace death if this was how she arrived at the ultimate destination.

"Pretty rough!" Revine called out.

"Almost there."

The flurry of monochromatic ferocity on the view screen lessened as they entered the shallower portion of the atmosphere, revealing a landscape of concentrated blacks, grays, and whites. This was typical of Hieruth, as well, with added textures she couldn't identify.

From the wavelength readings, however, there was a lot more to perceive.

Sensors identified a flat area of neutral gradation, meaning minimal surface cover, and Vui navigated toward the prospective landing site. Revine seemed to bounce in his seats, phalanges tapping a hyper rhythm against his restraints.

The ground approached with excess speed, but Vui had obsessively trained for this. There would always be variables out of her control, and to minimize that list meant she had to become a capable pilot in an accelerated period. Of course, her decreased fear pheromones had been a boon once more.

Hovering above the ground, Vui released the landing gear, and the ship made its accompanying sounds.

"Can we get out yet?" Revine asked immediately.

She chuckled, throat bobbing with the emotion, then fretted once more that he was too young for this mission, too eager. Could that get him killed? Might it get her killed? Either way, the mission would be considered a profound failure. She didn't want that, though to offer her life in pursuit of expanding her species' knowledge base was noble, likely far nobler than anything else, in her estimation.

"Give it some time, won't you?" Her tone was gentle, teasing.

She glanced back at him to spot the dark hue invading his frontal lobe, a sign of self-consciousness.

"Sorry."

"No need to apologize. I'm excited too, but we have to do this right." She snapped the required toggles into place—one to keep the ship's wavelength defense at nearly full, and another to track their locations in case the ship would have to recover them on autopilot—and unbuckled from her seat.

It was time to put on their suits. Revine assembled his in record time. Vui took a little longer, blaming her aging joints.

Revine led the way to the exit, his helmet sliding into place, the visor shading his features. She checked her own helmet, the sealing mechanism a hum in her ear, and opened the shuttle door. Her extremities strained against the seal, then eased as the door lifted.

The landscape formed in front of them, and their suits disagreed with the temperature at once. She sent her lower extremities to the suit gage, twirling the controls, and gestured to Revine to do the same.

"We will have to come back to the ship soon, or else the suits will start to weaken."

"What! How will we be able to properly search?" he said.

"We'll take short visits, Revine. Think about it this way: this is better than the environment being entirely inhospitable."

Revine huffed, falling into step beside her, companions moving down the ramp in unison.

Then her helmet registered an oddity.

"Something's off."

Revine glanced at her, his head bobbing.

"Can you..." She paused, thin lids moving over rounded, hexagonal eyes. "Do you see...?"

The silence following her uncertainty gelled around them, lush, *vivid*. Revine's mouth opened as he stumbled off the ship, and the land seemed to ooze around his presence, accepting his shape by bending its own. Vui tripped after him, unwilling to let her charge venture forth on his own, dreading he might disappear completely into the organic folds of this bizarre place.

"My eyes. Something is wrong," he whispered suddenly, and collapsed.

She agreed, but had no way to discover the cause, for she joined him on the ground. As they shrieked, she tunneled inward for solace from the sharp, deep pain. She shut her lids, but there was no relief. She tried to crawl closer to him but appeared to be stuck where she was currently sprawled.

This was the worst outcome, the one Alcāt feared, the one that had made her fellow Hieruthians look at her with disgust. How could she let the need to understand—to learn something wholly new—be louder than the need to self-preserve?

And to let a brilliant, determined youth attend?

Revine screamed somewhere, both too far away and not far enough to avoid this suffering, and the knowledge worsened her own, for she was responsible. She was his mentor, and she had led him astray.

There was a death in this pain that wound around her and didn't let go for many minutes. To surrender was not in her nature and so she thrashed her chorus of limbs, feeling how they struck at the sky above and the vegetation surrounding, pushing against the onrushing eclipse. It was focused like splinters in her eyes, and a wetness ruptured forth. And then there was a shattering stillness.

Vui clutched herself, cocooning in the only comfort she had known all her life. Breathing flowed like a waterway, cooling her overheated form, and relaxation soon crystalized. The sensation of abrasive and short vegetation rose under her prostrate form, accompanied by the smell of flowers to mimic something close to rotting.

After an unmeasured amount of time, both in the shift of solar positioning and the thrum of her internal clock, she opened her eyes.

"Revy," she said, crawling to where she believed his screams had originated. She blinked, squinting against something ferocious now inhabiting her vision.

"I'm here." His voice was cracked. "I can see again. Open your eyes, Vui."

She did so, and understood his statement at once. There was a spray of wavelengths, like a recently untangled mass of thread, but there were no words to describe them. She blinked, gasped, squinted, then spotted him and resumed her approach.

At last, she arrived at his side, peering at him through cracked lids, seeing the stain of moisture on his own face. But it had pigmentation unlike anything she had ever witnessed. Dark, worrisome.

"I see you. I mean… *see you*. You are covered in different shades. Busy shades." Revine rolled upright, focus darting around her.

She draped a hand on his shoulder, urgency in the taut prickle of her limbs. "As do I, but I can't explain what that means. Do you feel anymore pain?"

"Only an ache." His wonder infused his voice, tone turning like a light smear tripping over the edge of night.

Her consciousness reeled. "We are infected, somehow. Our suits have been infiltrated. There is a pollutant… or—"

He shook his head. "Not yet. I don't want to define it yet."

"Our mission." She tried to stand, swayed, and Revine stabilized her. "We are here to describe."

"We will." He gave her a gentle bump of a higher extremity on her shoulder, levity in his wet, leaking eyes. "For right now, let us experience. We are the first of the *jæn* to leave Hieruth. We are witnessing in an unknown manner. It is profound, altering. I'd really just like to get used to it first."

She surveyed him and noted that almost religious overture of his statement. It wasn't a characteristic trait in her eager young student, but he no longer *looked* characteristic, for the details of his body shone and warmed under her freshly widened visual receptacles. How could one's mind not shift when attending such a journey?

With a shrug, she agreed, the pulse of her nervousness higher than she was accustomed. But that wasn't intolerable, not when considering the circumstances.

Vision, once a gradation from density of shadow to absence of shadow, now roiled with new tumult on a planet of which she had previously only seen cosmological maps. She wished she could remove her helmet and taste the very air that appeared to dance with bewildering, and almost too bright, hues.

"What do we call this?" Revine pointed to a layered plant that reached above their head, the stem a visceral, complex texture compared to the shimmering and highly reflective quality of the leaves.

"Perhaps you can name it."

His ensuing smile rivaled that glow filling the sky, and Vui couldn't stop herself from smiling, too.

Niill'o expanded in front of them, roiling with winged creatures that flickered and sparkled, catching light and shooting it at them, and the two *jæn* watched as each one disappeared into the gathering of tall, thick plants. A furred being scooted to their right, blending almost too well into the landscape. Another, much larger, stood out starkly against a distant geologic formation.

She dared to look to her right, and spotted a massive, drooping, blooming growth that housed numerous small buzzing creatures. Sounds overlapped and blended, combatted for attention, and faded into obscurity. To comply with Revine's request of existing before quantifying, Vui had to shut down her usual drive for knowledge in favor of precaution and awareness, both already heightened.

"Is this how Hieruth looks? Are there wavelengths at home we don't observe?" Revine gestured to the cool surface of what appeared to be a liquid that gathered between tree roots. Of course, they couldn't tell yet whether these were actual trees, and she resisted the urge to take a sample.

"It's difficult to determine yet, but I am doubtful. If there were other wavelengths to perceive, perhaps we would have evolved the physical ability to detect them."

Revine nodded, mouth agape, the curve of his helmet marked with the blurred reflections of the world. There was a hot quality to a flower nearby, the pigmentation like a warning. As they passed, the components that might have been petals lurched in their direction. Danger, indeed, Vui concluded.

"And what happens..." He trailed off, sending a gloved hand closer to the soft, creamy protrusions of another plant, watching if it responded. It did, upper section twining around his digits, unveiling tightly bound leaves or petals or something else.

Silence stewed, as if he forgot his question.

"What happens if we return to Hieruth?" Vui prompted.

"Yes."

"I thought you didn't want to."

His lower extremities shifted his weight, considering, debating. "I'm not sure if I could ever live with myself knowing I had deprived *jæn* of such variety, such splendor. We can't keep this to ourselves! We can see so much more! I want to tell everyone, especially my siblings."

She ducked her head to the hide her expression. She didn't want him to feel embarrassed by his honesty, by the innocence of his mind, and richness of his heart. Her understanding blossomed as spiraling fungi-like growths bending under her feet. She had assumed he would be the one she'd had to force back home. It was increasingly clear this was no longer the case.

In truth, the moment she stepped onto this ground, she knew this would be her final residence, however spiritual—and confounding—in shape the awareness was. There was nothing for her to return to, and more, there was everything here, as long as she could get her suit to work using the emergency jettison pod in the ship. She would make sure Revine made it back into space, and she would send data for all her remaining years. And maybe another *jæn* team would come to Niill'o—perhaps even Revine—and she would be well.

Vui was precisely where she had always hoped to be. It wasn't a lab, nor a university classroom. It wasn't a conference, nor a research center. This planet was the opposite of loneliness, of feeling disconnected from the rest of her people. This was home.

Eventually, she straightened and managed her strongest voice.

"And you will inspire so many in the drive for knowledge, Revine, to never stop seeking, to always look a little harder."

He grinned and whirled around, head tilted upward. Vui watched, blinking through moisture, sorrow at having to say goodbye to him so soon stinging harsher than any expanded visual abilities. To distract herself, she removed a recorder from the pocket of her suit, and surreptitiously imaged the young scientist in awe of this fascinating realm so that she would forever have proof of this companion—another species outlier who chose curiosity and individuality over apprehension—who ventured into the depths of uncertainty with her, only to crave a return to the very world that criticized his choices.

She admired him and would miss his peculiar, baffling earnestness.

"Look at this!" he called, helmet grazing the edges of a plant. "The Committee on Flora and Reproduction will love the striation pattern!"

Vui followed him as he communicated his astonishment, gauging how soon they would have to return to the ship to give the suit's filtration system break, considering the challenge of how to survive on her own here.

Of all the lessons she had passed to Revine, at the core was her desire that he find connection. Her narcissistic assumption was that their academic fondness would be enough, that their unique similarities would carry them into a shared future. But it wasn't, and she had to accept that.

Niill'o gave him the drive and desire to connect, to spread knowledge, and that was a development to be proud of, despite how dissimilar it looked to her personal dream, sculpted and grasped for her whole life.

But how could a scientist project an out-of-date dream onto someone else, especially when reality held such fervid beauty all around them? She looked at Revine, enmeshed in his observations, and relaxed with the arrival of the universe's simplest answer.

Survival

It was out there. The *Excirilous*. A truly horrendous name, Andri decided, but she couldn't be too critical. Her parents had named her Andromeda, after all.

This was supposed to be a race. This was supposed to be her moment of triumph. Yet, a mysterious pulse had hit both their ships, draining power.

"How in the grace of the Polepian Channel is this possible?" Her accompanying blob cooed its sympathies. She patted the head-like surface, nuzzling the outer sides in its preferred manner, and released a sound of outrage. "We were so close to pulling in front." She slammed a fist onto the arm of her chair. "At least he's also stranded."

At that, her screen flashed with an incoming message. She bit her lip, sensing the origin and feeling decidedly disinterested in talking to him. But Blub cooed again.

"Fine. But if he's calling to gloat, I'm cutting him off."

Blub nodded as if in agreement.

"What do you want, Master Excirilous?" Her tone was intentionally snide. She didn't want to talk to this scumflyer. She only wanted to beat him.

"Well." There was an odd pause. "I'm stuck."

She huffed. "No shit."

"I see you are also stuck."

"Your observational skills are absolutely astounding. Get off this frequency."

"I prefer to have some company. Not all of us are lucky enough to enjoy the presence of your gooey companion."

"My companion is *not* gooey. It's gelatinous."

The sentient creature puffed out what might have been a chest.

"Sorry. I shouldn't be racist," he said, "But I did mean it in a nice way. I don't have a companion."

"That's because no one would tolerate you."

"Ouch." Another pause. "So we're stuck. What do we do?"

"We?" Her memory turned hot with images of his vicious competitiveness over the last five years, how he got the gold in 56% of their races (she had calculated it), and how aloof he always was toward her at social gatherings. It didn't help he'd also been one of those high-achieving students in their colony, one who seemed to excel without any effort.

She hated him. She would rather die than traipse into any kind of "we" status. The suggestion made her sick.

Andri cleared her throat, rallying her composure. "Well, *I* am going to mechanic my way out of this problem and win, obviously. Don't you wish you had taken more engineering classes?"

"I took plenty." His tone was uncharacteristically heavy. "To be honest..."

Multiple silent seconds ticked by. Andri grimaced in the interim. "To be honest *what*?"

"I'm kind of tired of this."

Her acerbic retort died in her throat.

"Aren't you?"

"Nope," she said at once.

"I know you hate me."

"True."

"But look over there. It's absolutely beautiful, right?"

Andri shot a breath upward that didn't budge her short, slightly sweaty bangs.

"Out there," she said mockingly. "You mean the endless expanse of space I'm already staring at? If you start talking about the stars, Mr. Excirilous, I will never race you again, and you will rue the day you got all poetic on your longest, most impressive rival."

"You are that," he said. She detected a baffling lack of sarcasm. "Look toward home, you asteroid."

That was usually a term to make fun of someone who wasn't aware, who was oblivious and annoying. And he'd called her that countless times.

But this utterance was different, almost warm. What was he up to? It was suspicious.

"Fine. I'm looking out into space instead of fixing the *Medallion*. Happy? I'm fully unprepared if you suddenly get control back and speed to the finish line."

"I won't do that."

"Sure." She trailed her attention to the right side of her screen and noted what he was talking about. "Oh."

"Yup. I could say something cliche about how we're always racing past life instead of looking at it..."

"But you most definitely won't do that, will you, Mr. Excirilous?" The disdain propelled her comment but hadn't made it to her voice. Instead, she sounded embarrassingly awed.

"Please stop calling me that."

"I won't call you anything else," she said.

Blub made a sound.

"Your gelatinous pet wants you to call me Ponty."

"Blub most definitely does not."

"Blub?" Ponty laughed. "That's a good name. So what do you think?"

"Of the stellar nursery you pointed out with all its layers of gorgeously colored gas?" She didn't want to give him too much credit. "It's fine."

"There's a lot that's fine out there."

"Are you getting old or something? You're all... sentimental."

His exhale was long. "My parents demanded I do one last race. I didn't want to. But we agreed. One last race."

Andri's shock clouded her thoughts. "Huh? What else would Ponty Therlyl do with his life?"

"Something like live. Actually live, Andromeda Gavol."

"Don't call me that."

"Okay. But only because you called me Ponty instead of that other name. Why do you even use it? Seems inconvenient to say out loud.."

Her brows stitched together. "It doesn't count if it's your full name to make a point."

"Fair."

Confused, she glared at comms, then pivoted to problem solving. Multiple minutes passed, and Andri immersed herself mechanical problem. After fiddling with everything accessible from the cockpit, she made progress. But without a spacesuit, she couldn't work on other parts of the ship, and of course she'd ditched any extra weight for the race.

It wasn't smart, really, this long-term consciousness-consuming urgency to beat this smug little shit. She hadn't really lived, she realized, and actually thumped a rounded fist on her panel that, perhaps, Ponty was a tiny bit right.

Damnit.

Blub gyrated on her shoulder as the screen registered improvement. To her surprise, she could manage small rushes of power, as if the fuel connection was faulty, going live then dying. If she could only travel by brief spurts, it would take a long time to cross the finish line.

"Polep's sake!" she yelped.

"I like when you curse."

Andri froze. She had forgotten—or plainly assumed—that their connection had ended.

"That's ridiculous. You don't like anything about me."

Ponty went quiet.

"You're really just that needy to hear someone's voice?"

"I don't like isolation." Noises sparked in the background, and he shrieked in pain.

She should feel a thrill of satisfaction knowing he had hurt himself. The only thing she felt was confusion about her emotional turmoil.

"I'm fine," he said, "though I know you weren't particularly concerned."

"Stop making it seem like you think you know me," she said.

Ponty resumed as if he hadn't heard her. "I think your ship's name is cool."

She scrunched up her face. Mind games! "My parents named it. I only inherited it. A pretty good family heirloom if you ask me."

"Agreed." He chuckled as he noisily worked. "But more specifically: *Medallion. Andromeda.* It's clever."

"They didn't name the ship after me. I wasn't even born yet." Why were they having this conversation? Why didn't she just shut him off?

Blub turned its body into a swirling curve, one of its favorite forms of entertainment in space. Andri smiled.

"Throw that theory away, then." She could almost hear a smile in Ponty's voice. "You were named after the ship."

To her irritation, she hadn't considered this. "Maybe. But it still seems like a stretch." She tapped her sensors, propping a leg over her arm rest. "What about yours?"

"An old story about an orphan who galaxy hopped until he

came to an unnamed planet. He decided to name it *Excirilous,* which in his language meant home.

"But." She was starting to tie thoughts together. "You said you're getting sick of racing. So the ship isn't really your home anymore if you want to leave it."

"This ship will always be my home. It's just how I use my home is probably going to change."

She stared at the nursery birthing new stars and stayed silent.

"I have power," Ponty said.

"Lucky you."

"No, I mean..." A cacophony came through their connection. "Only bursts, like that radiation knocked the injector loose, but at least it's not entirely severed."

I came to the same conclusion, she almost confessed.

"I have an idea."

She drooped in her worn seat. "What's stopping you? Off you go then. You know where the finish line is."

"The idea includes both of us, Andri."

"We? Both? What's going on with you?"

"I've been a real... what would you call me? A boil on Polep's ass?"

"That's actually exactly what I would call you."

Blub leapt into the air.

"That's what I'm tired of," he said. "Racing. Being an ass to everybody. Let's help each out of this."

Her eyes narrowed, though he couldn't see her. "I don't trust you, buddy."

"Then let me try to change that."

A song quietly arrived over the speaker, and she cocked her head. It was a ballad from their colony, one she had danced to with her parents.

"Why are you playing 'Bound Unbound' right now?"

"Because I remember you liked it."

She sat silently, letting the familiar notes gradually escalate. "Your memory is weird."

"It's possible I'm wrong. But you always smiled when you heard this come on. You have a nice smile."

That was enough. Ponty had been taken over by a strangely nice parasite. He had to have been.

"I suggest I grab the *Medallion*," he said, "and then you can take off from there. Hopefully, with the momentum, you'll get enough juice to keep going."

Wait. That was a solution that would solely benefit her. "Leave you here?"

"You can get help. A bigger ship will need to tow me back."

Blub slunk onto her thigh, turning its oblong upper half in her direction. She knew her gelatinous pal quite well. It was *pleading*.

Everything is wrong, she thought, and I'll never understand. "As much as I want to leave you here, Blub would be forever angry with me if I did that."

"Ahhh, the gelatin is fond of me."

"I wouldn't go that far!" She rumbled around her mind in search of a two-ship solution, which was right there in Ponty's own idea. "Okay, you grab me, fling me. I grab you, fling you. We just kind of... sling shot each other back."

A beat.

"Logical. But it'll take a while, and you don't like me."

"Honestly," she said, biting her lip, "it might be therapeutic to throw you around. And to clarify, I don't like the brash and inconsiderate and arrogant and *loud* racing champion Mr. Excilirious. Whoever Ponty Therlyl is, he's not so bad."

"I'm honored to be not too bad. You want to do the first fling?"

She grinned. "I really do. Strap in, Ponty."

Over the comms, the song ended, and she couldn't ignore the uptick in her heartrate. The plan felt logical, possible. She checked the engine and readied herself to throw the *Excirilous* like a goddamn ball of barn.

"You know what," she said cheerfully, "this is going to be fun."

She locked onto the ship, drew it back, then sent it hurtling in the direction of the distant finish line. The rush of pent-up adrenaline made her shriek with glee. Blub jostled and squeaked.

Breathless, Ponty checked in. "That level of force seemed a bit excessive, but I probably deserved it. Ready for your turn, Andri of the *Medallion*? I won't be so rough."

She raised a brow, mouth curving into a smirk. "As I've shown for the entirety of our lives, I can take anything you send my way."

"True," he said, tone ruffled with amusement. "On to the next stage, then."

Blub settled into Andri's pocket, trembling with excitement as the two rival ships tumbled through far-flung whispers of an eager nebula, their truce more thrilling than any win.

Engineering Marvels

The SaGoly sifted debris with its primary focus, an automatic effort, while leveraging the rest of his consciousness to listen for a song from the AfGoly. It had been quiet for a while, and usually at this stage in the solar rotation, AfGoly would send its regular update.

It wasn't a particularly communicative Goliath, but it had always been reliable.

SaGoly paused, assessing the pile of assorted detritus with minimal urgency. Its extensive Anthropogenic Era Inventory was perpetually engaged, and the system rapidly noted busted tires, ceramic shards, rotten diapers, beams used to erect the tallest structures ever made, and electronic chips from the smallest—all that remained of the before.

The Goliath's were the final human task, one that carried on long after *Homo sapiens* slipped into extinction.

The programmed task of the team of Goliaths was two-fold: one, to process and eliminate the damaging effluvium, and two, to preserve the beauty and important items at each continents centralized locations. At those sites, the items that survived collapse were secured and protected to represent the past, or for any future visitors to understand the previous epoch.

Of course, whatever future visitors would *also* have to encounter the Goliaths, and it felt dishonest to present a world free of any signs of the before damage. But, SaGoly concluded, the damage was profound and likely would take several centuries to remedy—if the machines lasted that long.

While it moved steadily eastward in its efforts, SaGoly's receiver winked its reception directly into an internal awareness chamber.

NaGoly wafted a sudden song, like the orange rays of sunset across the upheaval of this previous city. SaGoly stopped moving and listened, allowing the sounds to filter inside the central processing unit for meaning retrieval.

EuGoly checked in earlier. It observed one of the ocean Goliaths nearing the shoreline. It was slowing down with weight. I wish they would talk to us. Maybe it needs help unloading.

SaGoly considered a song reply and then prepared it for transference into the upper atmosphere, reviewing the content as it released. *If you begin your travel now, perhaps you would make it only a few weeks too late, rather than months.*

NaGoly must have been especially attentive, for its response came within moments.

You think your humor is an asset. It is not. Perhaps you should find scrap to make wings. Then you could fly to help us, too, you lazy lug.

The messages carried amusement, and SaGoly rumbled its pleasure. Out of all the Goliaths, these two were the most bonded, though none of them understood why such a relationship would develop.

Once, AnGoly—the smallest of them all and most prone to rumination—shared a theory that the engineers had designed the two of them that way. That wasn't long before AnGoly said it was planning to float across the Drake Passage on the leftover metal from the dilapidating science station and meet SaGoly. There wasn't anything left to clean up in its region, AnGoly had said in a song like grief, and it had done a multitude of geographical inspections before the decision was made. AnGoly yearned for *more*, singing this truth to the entire fleet of Goliaths.

That was the last any Goliath heard of AnGoly, but the southern ocean Goliath reported finding pieces of familiar metal on the nearby shoreline.

Singing to each other, as they had discovered early on, was the only option to combat machine loneliness.

You know how I dislike heights, NaGoly. But I believe sufficient metal quantities exist in my currently inhabited region for the creation of a land-based vehicle, so perhaps there is still a way, if you are exceedingly patient.

SaGoly filled the quiet that returned this sustained jest with further material processing. Sometimes the coded drive to perform their duties overcame everything else, most of all bonding. And yet, the ability to communicate was integral to their systems.

Another mystery, but one SaGoly favored.

Eventually, NaGoly sang another thought. *I find too many beautiful things. My inventory does not like my ratio of secure vs. process.*

SaGoly dug deeper into the mound of trash. *I experience the same discomfiture. It is as though the inventory has a certain set of parameters that is increasingly narrow as time passes.*

NaGoly made a higher-range sound that carried no vocabulary, then added, *The Preservation Facilities are getting full.*

Indeed, SaGoly replied.

Neither sang for the remainder of the diurnal round, but both held this truth with trepidation.

What would they do when the Preservation Facilities were full? There would still be much to preserve from the past. Perhaps that was why the inventory sent repeated messages to SaGoly's communication center rejecting duplicate and redundant items it identified.

It had left behind so much already. Anything more could not be tolerated. And yet, another need formed in the spark-hiss of SaGoly's consciousness. It would one day soon leave its continent behind, traveling south, and never peer upon this landscape again.

Like Angola, they had all talked about leaving their continents, despite the need insurmountable challenge of departing their realms, and joining as one Goliath pod to resume their task of eliminating. But programming was a difficult drive to ignore, and none of them, save for AnGoly, had found the strength—or desperation—to attempt it.

As evening claimed SaGoly's domain, it imagined dawn was just beginning for AuGoly and AsGoly. Of course, neither of them liked to rest, preferring to eliminate and preserve through all hours in an indefinite race against each other. With this in mind, SaGoly sent a song of consideration to both, a nudge of *I am thinking of you, family members.* Overhead, the clouds sped up, wafting and contorting with the wind.

Then, a quiet, harmonious nudging reached the Goliath.

I have grown slower. I no longer track the days well. But I have made progress, nonetheless.

A surge of relief sputtered through SaGoly's burbling brain.

AfGoly? I was worried.

There is no need to worry. I will continue my task for many years yet.

SaGoly sent a responding twill of agreement and happiness. *I missed you. Please do not go silent like that.*

AfGoly took several moments to respond. *Silence is a comfort. The song of us no longer sounds so sweet.*

You are melancholy, AsGoly sang quietly. *I would show you a lovely dawn now, but I know it will reach you eventually.*

AuGoly chirped, its resonance warm. *What is it like, family, to be living in our past?*

We all inhabit the past, NaGoly rumbled, and the Goliaths continued their ceaseless efforts.

Semantically this was true, and yet they each would reach for a future wherein their saved items would be viewed and treasured as artifacts from an alien race. And in that epoch, the past would sound like behemoths crunching the devastated landscapes into plains for new life to grow, of mechanical choruses that circulated the planet like breezes.

Thank you for spending time with these characters.

Please leave a review on Amazon, Goodreads, or Barnes & Noble. Such support means a lot to a self-published author!

Visit BrianeWillis.com to see my other genre-bending books, including *A Mythology Woven*, which is a collection of short stories inspired by fantasy and fairytales. You can also join my newsletter to receive title reveals, art peeks, and upcoming projects.

www.ingramcontent.com/pod-product-compliance
Lightning Source LLC
Chambersburg PA
CBHW070752120626
46557CB00002B/554